BADGER THURSTON and the Runaway Stagecoach

BY
GUS BRACKETT

ILLUSTRATIONS BY
DON GILL

VALLEY of the TETONS
LIBRARY
Victor
votlib.org

Twelve Baskets Book Publishing
Three Creek, Idaho

Twelve Baskets Book Publishing, LLC
48600 Cherry Creek Rd.
Rogerson ID 83302
www.12bookbaskets.com
gus@12bookbaskets.com

ISBN 978-0-9841876-2-1

Other books in this series

Badger Thurston and the Cattle Drive

Table of Contents

Illustrations

Map

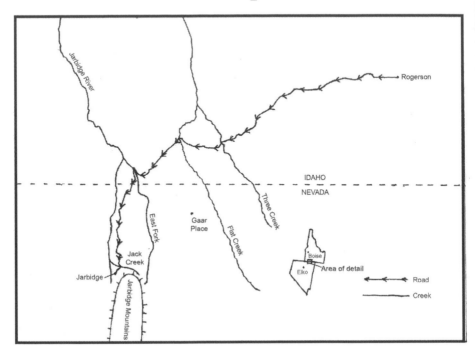

Chapter One

The stagecoach groans to a stop at the top of a steep grade. Badger Thurston grabs the edge of his seat as he peeks into the deep canyon. He holds onto a shotgun as he traces the winding two-track road down the canyon side into the narrow canyon and back out the other side. Fear slowly rises from the pit of his stomach and travels up through his face.

The stagecoach driver sitting next to Badger looks at him with a half-crazed grin and says, "Now's a good time to pray."

The driver, Frank Newton, flicks the reins, and the stagecoach tips down the steep road. The brown boulders at the side of the road whiz past Badger. The frightened teen adjusts his grip on the seat and double-barreled shotgun as the stagecoach approaches a grove of aspen trees tucked behind a sharp corner.

"Shouldn't you slow down?" Badger asks.

"The horses can't slow the coach," Frank says.
"We just have to stay out in front of it."

Frank shakes the reins, which are wound around
his fingers. The horses trot slightly faster now. Badger

reaches for where a brake would be if it were on his side of the coach.

A woman inside the passenger compartment asks, "Can't you make this insufferable stagecoach move any smoother, Mr. Newton?"

"No," Frank says. "In fact, it's about to get rougher. Everyone, lean right."

Badger leans his head, neck, and chest to the right as the horses and stagecoach career around the tight curve. The steep road suddenly becomes steeper, and the stagecoach picks up even more speed. Badger feels lightheaded but holds tightly to the gun and his seat.

"Hold on, everyone!" Frank yells as he pulls on the reins to stop the horses and yanks up on the brake lever. But the stagecoach doesn't slow down. The brake smells like a campfire and whines loudly with strain.

"Frank! Frank, we're goin' too fast!" Badger cries out.

"Shut up," Frank says without raising his voice. "Lean left, everyone."

Badger leans to the left and sits deeper in his splintery seat. The team and stagecoach hug a corner like painted horses on a merry-go-round, and the road levels slightly. Frank shakes the reins again, and the horses pick up a little more speed. Just as Badger begins to relax, one of the wagon's front wheels hits a rock, jolting the coach and throwing Frank and Badger up in the air. Within moments, both thud back down into their seats. Badger loses his grip on the shotgun. It slides toward the ground, but Badger manages to snatch it back. He pulls the gun to his side and cradles it in his arms.

"Better not lose that," Frank says with a smile. "You should at least look like you're guardin' the coach."

The stagecoach levels out and then bumps over a slight hill, picking up speed on the decline. Badger feels like a passenger on a Coney Island roller coaster.

"Lean left. Lean left hard," Frank yells.

Badger leans left as the stagecoach tracks the horses around another steep crook in the trail. The two left wheels come up off the ground, and Badger feels the stagecoach tipping dangerously.

"Hyah, hyah," Frank calls to the team as he flaps the reins again.

The horses lunge forward, and the stagecoach wobbles back to the ground. The thin steel straps around the outside of the wheels cut through the dust, and the wheels' spokes spin like pinwheels in a windstorm. The road, slightly wider than two horses standing side by side, finally flattens out. Frank pulls back on the reins, and the two brown horses and the two coppery-red, or sorrel, horses slow to a trot, then walk, and then stop. Frank looks at Badger and chuckles. Badger leans his head over the edge of the stagecoach and barfs up his lunch.

"Mr. Newton, I am telling your supervisor about your reckless driving," a woman says from the passenger cabin.

"Please do," Frank says. "My dad's my supervisor, and I've been tryin' to quit for years now. I'd owe you one if I got fired."

Frank waggles the reins, and the stagecoach lunges forward. The stagecoach follows the narrow road down a short hill. The baby-faced Frank steers the horses into a small meadow next to a clear creek. Frank stops the stage and jumps from his perch. The two passengers stumble out of the coach and take deep breaths.

"We'll rest here for a bit," Frank says. "The water's drinkable, and there are no rattlesnakes, if you wanna rest in the grass."

Badger climbs down from his seat. He reaches the ground and wobbles. The slightly pudgy teen wipes his sleeve across his mouth and then helps Frank unharness the horses.

BADGER STOKES A SMALL campfire that dances around a bubbling pot of coffee. Nearby, the horses graze on the short meadow grasses lining the tree-shaded creek. Small groves of trees dot the canyon floor, but only short sagebrush grows on the canyon's sides. As the afternoon sun makes its slow descent, aspen trees and the towering canyon wall cast shadows across the entire area.

"Coffee's ready," Badger says.

Frank is the first to grab a cup of coffee. He sits down and watches the steam rise from his cup, but he does not drink. Badger sets out two empty cups for the passengers.

Johnny Greene is tall and tan. His dark hair frames sharp features. His shirt is whiter than any white shirt Badger has ever seen, and it is as stiff as wax paper. He is well dressed in a black dress coat, red vest, and neatly shaped black hat. He wears tailored, black leather gloves. They're not riding or working gloves; in fact, they look a lot like ladies' gloves. Badger thinks it's strange that Johnny doesn't have a pistol and his clothes were made without buttons. All the same, he suspects ladies would describe the gambler as handsome.

The other passenger is as pretty as Johnny is handsome. Madeline Dubois's dark-red hair is tucked beneath a fancy hat. She wears a long, flowing silk dress that is covered in lace and frills. Her blouse looks too tight. Her boots are shiny white and seem too small to be comfortable. Badger wonders if all her fashion is why she is always so unpleasant.

"I would prefer a spot of tea," Mrs. Dubois says as she looks down her nose at Badger.

"Sorry, ma'am, we only have coffee," Badger says.

"Then I will have cream and sugar with my coffee," Mrs. Dubois says. "And freshen up your repulsive brew with some ground nutmeg and cinnamon."

Badger looks at her like a dog watches a fireworks display. He scratches his head and says, "I ... uh ... we don't have ... what was it again?"

"Cream and sugar, you fool."

"No problem, Mrs. Dubois," Frank says with an impish grin. "I'll milk the goat, and Badger'll run down to the general store for the sugar."

"There's no general store, Frank," Badger says.

"We have coffee, black, and that's all, ma'am," Frank says.

"You are all insolent. *Vous avez cuillères dans le nez*," Mrs. Dubois says to Frank in French.

"You have spoons in your nose?" Johnny asks as he accepts a cup of coffee from Badger. "Is that a French insult I'm not familiar with?"

"Why, Mr. Greene, I did not realize you were an educated man. And, yes, it is a common insult."

"Don't mind Mrs. Dubois, boys," Johnny says to Frank and Badger. "She tries to speak French to sound sophisticated. But she used to live on a pig farm down in the valley. Her husband traded a side of bacon for a mine claim, and they found gold in the mine. So don't let her hoity-toity attitude fool you."

"Insolence! You are all vile reprobates," Mrs. Dubois says as she climbs into the stagecoach.

"I think Mrs. Dubois is right," Frank says as he pours out his coffee. "It's time to go."

6

Johnny tips his head back and gulps down the thick liquid as Badger dumps the coffeepot's remaining brew on the fire. Badger collects the utensils and then helps Frank ready the wagon. The two quickly harness the horses. They buckle straps and pull leather through rings. The setup confuses Badger, but Frank seems to work almost without thinking. A gentle breeze rustles the trees' leaves. Frank and Badger climb up the stage and sit on the driver's long, bench-like seat.

"I've got a question, Frank," Badger says.

"What is it, rookie?" Frank replies.

"Well, I know I'm supposed to guard the stagecoach. And I know you gave me a shotgun. But you didn't give me any bullets. How am I supposed to guard anything without bullets?"

"Shh! Not so loud," Frank whispers. "You're supposed to look like you're guardin' the stage. That should be enough to scare someone from tryin'. Besides, you keep throwin' that gun around. If it were loaded, it could go off and really hurt someone. We don't want that."

"So let me get this straight," Badger says. "I'm just an actor."

"That's right. And the better you act, the safer we'll be."

Badger shakes his head as Frank rustles the reins, and the stage jumps to a start.

"Up and down one more hill, and we're in Jarbidge," Frank says with a smile. "And even though Crippen Grade is tricky, it's the easiest part of the trip."

THE HORSES GASP in the thin mountain air as they walk to the grade's top. Frank keeps the reins still as he speaks simple commands to the horses and clicks his tongue. The stagecoach moves slower than the cloud of dust it is kicking up. As Badger watches, the cloud paints them all in a thin, white layer of grime.

As the coach reaches the hilltop and levels out, a knock sounds on the roof of the passenger compartment.

"Driver," Johnny calls from below Badger and Frank. "Driver, I need to stop."

"No stops," Frank replies. "We're already behind schedule."

"Driver, it is important. I'd even say it's necessary that we stop."

"Why's that, Mr. Greene?" Frank asks.

"I need to talk to a man about a horse," Johnny says slowly.

"There are no horse traders up here, mister," Frank says with a devious smile and wink at Badger as the stage continues across the hill's flat top.

"It's not that, Frank," Johnny says. "I need to shake hands with the mayor."

"The mayor of what, Crippen Grade?" Frank replies, chuckling.

"I need to pay some rent on the coffee I drank," Johnny says, almost pleading.

"You need to what?" Frank asks. "Why don't you just say it?"

"I need to pee," Johnny says loudly. "I was trying to be discreet in the presence of Mrs. Dubois, but I need to pee."

"Right on schedule," Frank says with a grin. "The coffee we had at the meadow usually shakes down by now. It's a predictable part of this trip. There's a grove of trees just up here."

As the team passes the grove of white-barked aspen trees, Frank pulls back on the reins, and the horses stop. One of the four horses paws the ground and nods his head. Johnny fumbles with the cabin's latch until the door finally pops open. He climbs down and walks quickly to the trees.

Frank sits in his seat with the reins relaxed on the dashboard. He whistles a happy tune. Frank is about ten years older than Badger. He is too old to be called a kid, but he's not quite old enough to be considered a man. Frank Newton has a forgettable face. *If you saw him on a street in town,* Badger thinks to himself, *you would forget what Frank looks like before you reached the next block.*

Frank pulls his little gray hat back to wipe the sweat from his forehead. He wipes his face with his gray scarf and unbuttons the bottom button on his gray vest. Frank is of average height and average weight. His blond hair isn't long, but it's too long to be called short.

Badger looks around the hilltop for robbers. The teen shifts back and forth as his head pivots from side to side. He feels as uneasy as a little boy at a tea party. Badger raises the shotgun as he scans the grove.

Badger's real name is Lawrence, but everyone calls him Badger because he looks so much like a badger. He has a long nose, round cheeks, and big front teeth. His little bit of pudge jiggles when he walks.

"Put that gun down," Frank says. "It's empty, remember? If you wave it around, you could get shot."

"I don't like carryin' this shotgun without any ammunition in it," Badger says.

"Well, that's what I hired you to do," Frank says. "I want you to look like you're guardin' the stage, but I don't want anyone gettin' hurt."

"What am I guardin' that's so important?"

"Well, Badger, this is a mail wagon. Sometimes, we carry bags full of letters, periodicals, and other packages to all the little ranches between Rogerson and Jarbidge. Other times, we carry cash for all the payroll at the mines."

"Is this one of those 'other' times?" Badger asks.

"Maybe," Frank says with a knowing look as he peers up at the wispy clouds.

The horses fidget in their harnesses, and the stagecoach moves slightly. Suddenly, a shot booms from behind Badger. The horses jump, and Frank grabs for the reins. Badger smells gun smoke, so he raises the shotgun and looks behind him. A second shot fires, and Badger's ears ring. The lead horses rear up on their hind legs and then lunge forward. The stagecoach lurches forward and bumps the back pair of horses. Then all the horses lunge and run down the road. Frank pulls back on the reins, but the horses bite their bits, ignoring Frank's command to stop. Badger clutches the shotgun with one hand and hangs onto the speeding wagon with the other.

"Whoa! Whoa!" Frank hollers as he yanks on the reins to cue the horses to stop.

The horses and coach charge down the road through another grove of trees. Frank leans right to avoid a low branch. The normally cool driver looks scared for the first time since they left Rogerson this morning. Badger leans left as the stagecoach races toward a thick limb. As he straightens, a low-hanging branch slaps Badger in the chest and forces him to the edge of his seat. Badger loses his balance, so he grabs Frank. Instead of stopping his fall, both Badger and Frank topple from their perch. They crash to the ground in a rolling heap of limbs. As the stagecoach speeds away, Frank and Badger fall still. Their eyes are closed, and their breathing is shallow. The runaway stagecoach shoots up a long plume of dust as it speeds along the road like a rabbit with its tail on fire.

Chapter Two

Badger opens his blue eyes. He is lying on a bunk in a dark, damp room. The air smells like a smoky cookstove. Badger closes his eyes. His head is throbbing. Badger feels as queasy as a land lover on a deep-sea fishing boat. He feels a bump on his skull just above his left ear. Badger opens his eyes and looks around the concrete room again. From one corner of the dark structure, Johnny Greene awkwardly strikes a match. Strangely, Johnny holds the match between his middle and ring finger.

"Mornin', Badger," Johnny says.

"Where are we?" Badger asks.

"We're in the Jarbidge Jail," Johnny replies.

"Jail? What did I do?" Badger asks as he rubs his head. "The last I remember, the horses were runnin' away. I got hit by a branch, and then I can't remember anything else."

Badger blinks and yawns. He rubs his sleepy eyes and tenderly touches the bump on his head.

Johnny's neat vest is open, and Badger notices again that his vest doesn't have any buttons.

"Well, Badger, that's my problem, too," Johnny says. "I left for a minute, and when I returned, the stage was gone. I found you and Frank a few hundred yards down the road. You were both knocked out."

"So where is Frank?" Badger asks.

"They took Frank to the doctor's office. The sheriff said most everyone here in town heard two shots get fired. Since you were the only person carryin' a gun, he brought you to the jail," Johnny says.

"But I didn't fire the shots. They can't just put me in jail for carryin' a shotgun ... can they?" Badger asks.

Johnny takes a deep breath and looks at the morning sunlight streaming through a seam between the sheets of tin on the ceiling. "Well, the mail was stolen from the coach. The mail, Sheriff Blakely told me, included $1,800 in payroll. The sheriff thinks either you or I stole it. He thinks we might be in cahoots."

"But I barely know you," Badger says. "How could we be in cahoots?"

"That's just what he's sayin'."

Badger scratches his head and looks at Johnny. Badger is annoyed that he has been tied to Johnny Greene. *He's a drifter and gambler and probably also a thief,* Badger thinks. *It's obvious why Johnny is here, but why am I in jail?*

As Badger stares blankly at the dark walls, steel keys jingle and the steel door creaks open. Candlelight flickers dimly into the cell, and a man with two-day-old gray stubble sticks his head through the doorway. His hair is not combed, and his shirt is partially untucked. A button is missing on his vest, and a sweat ring rims his brown hat. His boots are scuffed, but all his clothes are clean and pressed.

12

"Badger Thurston," the man says, "your bail's been posted. You're free to go till your hearing tomorrow."

Badger grabs his hat and steps into the candlelit sheriff's office.

The Jarbidge Jail is small and looks temporary, like it was thrown together using materials that were just lying around. Two outside walls are rock, and the other two are concrete. The roof is flimsy tin. The inside of the square building is flat concrete, and a steel-barred interior wall with a steel-barred door separates the single jail cell from the sheriff's office. Inside the cell, two small bunks are attached to opposite walls. A three-gallon bucket squats in one corner and smells like an outhouse. Badger wonders if that is where jailbirds are supposed to pee, but he doesn't want to stay in jail long enough to find out. The building has no windows, so the only light that creeps in comes from holes and cracks in the poorly made structure.

Badger closes his eyelids in a long blink. When he opens them, he sees the shadowy form of Percy Reed sitting at the sheriff's desk filling out paperwork.

"What are you doin' here?" Badger asks Percy.

"The sheriff sent a rider to my dad's store in Three Creek to tell him the stage wouldn't be drivin' back through or returnin' to Rogerson anytime soon. Dad asked a few questions and found out you were a suspect in the robbery. So here I am, postin' your bail," Percy sneers at Badger. "The sheriff wants $25 to make sure you show up at your hearin' Thursday."

"Why am I in jail?" Badger asks, "and where'd you come up with $25?"

"Well, kiss my cheek and call me smitten. That *is* a good question," Sheriff Blakely says. "Where does a kid come up with $25? Were you in on the robbery?"

13

"I'm not in on anything," Percy says. "I earned $30 on a cattle drive. I invested that money in a wagonload of watermelons. Those melons brought in $65. I bought a couple bushels of apples and then sold them for $98. It's amazin' how much money you can generate from a few good investments."

"That still doesn't answer my question," Badger says as he lifts his arms, palms up. "What's goin' on?"

"You've been arrested in the stagecoach's robbery," the sheriff says in a slow drawl. "There's $1,800 in payroll missin'. You and Johnny Greene are the primary suspects."

"Why am I a suspect?" Badger asks. "'I was tryin' to guard the stage, not rob it."

"Durin' my investigation, I discovered that only four people were in the area at the time of the robbery," the sheriff says. "And those four people were with the stagecoach. Frank Newton isn't a suspect. The Newtons own the stagecoach, and Frank wouldn't steal from his own family. Besides, Frank's unconscious over at Doc Bettis's office. Meanwhile, the Dubois family owns Elkorah Mine. The stolen money was supposed to pay that mine's workers. Madeline Dubois isn't gonna steal from her own husband. That leaves you and Johnny Greene at the scene, which makes you the primary suspects. You're free to go, but don't go too far. You have a date with the justice of the peace."

"But, Sheriff, aren't you the justice of the peace?" Percy asks.

"Only on Thursdays. I'm sheriff on Mondays, Wednesdays, and Fridays. I'm fire marshal on Tuesdays, and I tend bar at the Mint on weekends."

"Boy, Sheriff, is there any job you *don't* do in this town?" Badger asks.

"Mayor. I'm not the mayor. I hate politics."

Sheriff Blakely opens the door, and Badger and Percy walk out.

"What's your plan, Badger?" Percy asks.

"Whattaya mean?"

"If I know you, you're plannin' something."

"I don't have a plan yet, Percy. But I need to find out who robbed the stagecoach, and I need to know by Thursday."

"Where should we start?" Percy asks.

"Let's head back up the grade and see if we can pick up any clues," Badger says as he turns on his heel and walks toward the livery stable.

BADGER AND PERCY PULL up their horses and dismount. Percy rides old, dependable Snowball, and Badger rides a horse named Jo that Percy rented for him at the livery stable. From their lofty position at the top of Crippen Grade, the boys can see the town of Jarbidge in the distance below.

Percy tips his new gray hat back off his forehead. His blue shirt and blue pants hang loosely on his scrawny body. While Badger looks like a badger, Percy looks more like a weasel—very thin and not very tall. The young cowboys begin surveying the area where the stagecoach had stopped as it waited for Johnny to do his business. A curious Badger studies the wagon tracks and hoofprints on the road. He follows the trail like a coyote tracking a jackrabbit. Badger picks up a shiny, black rock and turns it over twice. He squats down and fidgets with the rock again before tossing it over his shoulder.

"What are we lookin' for?" Percy asks.

"I have no idea, Percy," Badger replies as he turns toward the grove. "But we have to find some evidence that proves I'm innocent."

"So what would prove your innocence?" Percy asks as he lifts his hat and scratches his head.

"I don't know."

"Badger, look down the road. Somebody's comin'."

Badger squints at the canyon side. "I can't see him," he says as he leans forward. "Who is it?"

"I can't make him out either. But I don't want him to know we're up here," Percy says. "Let's hide in those trees and see what he's up to."

Badger and Percy lead their horses to the nearby grove. They tie Snowball and Jo to low branches and settle themselves into a well-hidden patch of brush.

A lone, seemingly nervous horseman rides cautiously up the trail and looks around like a detective searching for clues.

"Badger, is that Frank Newton?" Percy asks in a whisper.

"It can't be. He got thumped in the accident and has been unconscious since then," Badger says as he lifts his hat and scratches his head.

"Well, take a look. If it isn't him, it could sure be his brother. He's got the same face, same brown eyes, same gray hat, gray vest, and gray pants—even the same hairstyle."

"I hear you, Percy, but that's an awful quick recovery if it is him."

"But you had the same fall, and here you are," Percy reminds Badger

"Yeah, but I wasn't hurt enough to go to the doctor," Badger says.

The rider dismounts near the edge of the grove in which Badger and Percy are hiding. He strides to a prickly bush covered in tree branches. The man who looks like Frank reaches into the bush, winces in pain, and pulls out three white canvas bags. "US Mail" is stamped on the bags in black letters. The unknown rider returns to his horse, ties the bags to his saddle, and swings onto the animal's back. He pulls his horse around and rides quickly down the road.

"Should we follow him?" Percy asks.

"Yeah, but let him get down the road a little bit first."

As the man rides out of sight, Badger and Percy hurry to Jo and Snowball. They slide into their saddles and jog their horses along the roadside's grass and brush to limit the amount of dust they kick up. Without saying a word, the boys ride just out of sight of the Frank-Newton-lookalike.

The man follows the trail through a stand of white-barked aspen trees and around a bend. Just past a rocky outcropping, he stops abruptly, dismounts sloppily, and pulls a small shovel from behind his saddle. He unties two of the three bags. With loot and tool in hand, he disappears behind the boulders.

"What's he doin'?" Percy asks quietly.

"I can't be certain," Badger says, "but I bet he's buryin' the money."

Badger and Percy dismount and tie their horses to some sagebrush. The young cowboys crouch behind a patch of brush where they can see the rider but are hidden from him. The man works quickly, pausing occasionally to look around like a ground squirrel in hawk country. He digs a shallow hole, deposits the money, and throws dirt on top of the bags. He grabs some brush and sticks to put on top of the freshly covered hole. The unknown rider scans the area and strides quickly back to his horse. In one motion, he grabs the reins and swings onto his horse. The rider looks over his shoulder one more time and then gallops down the trail. As his cloud of dust drifts away, Badger and Percy approach the two buried sacks.

"What now, Badger?" Percy asks.

"Well, we need those bags, and we need to follow that rider to see where he's goin',"

Badger says. "Why don't you follow the rider while I dig up those bags?"

"Oh no, Badger," Percy says with a scowl. "I'm not followin' him. He's probably armed and would probably see me comin' at some point."

Badger shakes his head. "Okay, okay. I'll follow the rider while you get the mailbags."

Percy takes a deep breath and sighs. "How about we both dig up the mail and then follow the rider together? I think we're better off when we stick together."

"All right, but let's hurry. That skunk already has a head start."

The two young cowboys pull away the brush, and each grabs a stick to use as a makeshift shovel. The disturbed dirt is soft and moves easily. Badger and Percy dig up the bags in about half the time it took the thief to bury them. They pull the bags out and hurry back to their horses.

"No time to count it, Percy. Just tie that bag to your saddle, and let's get goin'."

Each of the boys secures a bag to his saddle. They mount up and ride a short distance to where the road overlooks Jarbidge. Badger and Percy stop their horses and search for the rider in town.

Jarbidge is a mining boomtown that hugs the mountainside in the bottom of a canyon. Several little mining shacks line its single, dirt-packed street. There are dozens of businesses—general stores, mercantiles, restaurants, and hardware stores—more businesses than a town the size of Jarbidge should have. The Nevada Hotel is the town's grandest building. Jarbidge's Commercial Club, while functional, is still under construction. Its school is half-filled with children. A handful of tents flap on the edge of town, but no one in Jarbidge will spend another winter living in a tent.

19

"Do you see the thief, Percy?" Badger asks as he stands in his stirrups and stretches his neck to get a better look.

"Right there," Percy says, pointing toward the main street. "I'm pretty sure that's him."

In the distance, the rider dismounts and talks to a boy who takes the short bay horse's reins and walks away. The thief wraps his coat around the mailbag and enters the Nevada Hotel.

"What's he doin', Badger?" Percy asks.

"Beats me, Percy. But let's see what's in these bags. We might have the evidence we need to clear my name."

Chapter Three

"... ONE THOUSAND ONE HUNDRED ninety-eight ... one thousand one hundred ninety-nine ... one thousand two hundred," Badger says as he places the final dollar on top of a green stack of bills.

"How much did you say was stolen?" Percy asks.

"I think it was $1,800 in missin' payroll," Badger replies. He draws a math problem in the dirt at the side of the road where he counted the money. "So we're $500 short of the total," Badger says with a pained grimace.

"We're $600 short, unless the sheriff's math skills are as bad as yours," Percy says with a chuckle. "So how do we get the last $600?"

"I don't have any idea, Percy, but this should start to clear my name. And I'll bet that rider has the rest of the money."

"I'm sure you're right, Badger. Let's take this money to the sheriff and see if we can straighten this out."

BADGER AND PERCY STORM into the sheriff's office lugging the two bags of money. The sheriff is half-asleep but wakes quickly, jumping to his feet. The friends sling the bags onto the desk in the dimly lit room.

"Well, pinch my cheek and call me a cutie. Whatta we got here, boys?" the sheriff asks as he strokes the stubble on his chin.

"Two-thirds share of the missin' payroll," Percy says from behind Badger.

"We found where it was hidden," Badger says. "And a rider who looks like Frank Newton walked into the Nevada Hotel with another bag about fifteen minutes ago. If you go down there—"

"Boys, I saw Frank Newton down at Doc Bettis's office just this mornin'. He was clingin' to life and in no condition to travel. I've got a hunch you two just had a fit of conscience and are bringin' your loot back."

"No, Sheriff, that's not it at all! We trailed a rider and watched him bury this money," Badger pleads.

"Tell it to the judge, son," Sheriff Blakely says with a sneer. "You were the only one carryin' a gun, and now you two haul in some of the stolen money. If I were judge, I'd say the evidence you brought in is enough to convict."

"But you are the judge," Percy says.

"Not till Thursday," the sheriff replies.

The sheriff gently grabs Badger and Percy by the shoulders and guides them into the jail cell. He closes the steel door with a *clang* and locks it with his key.

"And there'll be no bail this time, boys," the sheriff says with a sullen grin.

A MATCH STRIKES IN the corner of the jail cell, jumping to life and illuminating Johnny Greene's face. He holds the glowing stick between his fingers and touches it to a cigarette hanging loosely from his lips. Johnny inhales deeply and blows a plume of smoke from his mouth. The cloud drifts over to Badger and Percy.

Their eyes water, and Badger coughs like a chimney sweep at the end of his workday.

"Back already?" Johnny asks. "Did you find what you were lookin' for?"

"We found two-thirds of the missin' money," Percy says.

"And somebody who looks like Frank Newton carryin' a US mailbag into the Nevada Hotel," Badger says.

"Where were you supposed to stay here in Jarbidge, Mr. Greene?" Percy asks.

"Well, I had a room made up for me at the Nevada Hotel, until I was invited to stay in these fine accommodations," Johnny says as he casts a sour look at the pee bucket.

"So the rider with the money bag was lookin' for you," Badger says.

"Now don't be so quick to accuse," Johnny says calmly. "You two were the ones who strolled into the sheriff's office with $1,200."

"Yeah, but I didn't have a room at the Nevada Hotel. And I didn't have the stage stop right before it ran away."

"You don't have to convince me, Badger," Johnny says. "You have to convince the judge."

"But I'm innocent," Badger whines.

"Tell the judge," Johnny says with a grin. "Tell the judge, Badger."

UP IN THE HIGH country, time moves slowly. But inside a jail cell, it can seem like time isn't moving at all. Badger stares angrily at the concrete wall, and Percy sits with his arms around his knees to keep warm. The sun has been down for hours, but neither Badger nor Percy is tired. Sleep would be a welcomed escape, but the young jailbirds' eyes aren't weary.

24

Suddenly, Johnny jumps out of a bunk. He tucks in his shirt and straightens his collar. Badger thinks it's strange that the carefully dressed man doesn't wear a tie—not a bow tie, not a wild rag, not even those silly little string ties gamblers like to wear. Johnny's glove-covered hands place his hat on his head and tip it just right.

Badger eyes Johnny. "What are you gettin' all dressed up for?"

"As much fun as it is here," Johnny says with a cocky grin, "I have dinner and adult libations awaitin' me at the Nevada Hotel. If this cell is as cheaply made as all the others I've been in—"

Johnny steps onto a bunk and pushes a fist against the tin roof. With very little strain, the roof rises nearly two feet.

Johnny turns to Badger and Percy, "And it is cheaply made. Enjoy your evenin', boys—without me."

With that, Johnny stands as tall as he can and places his forearms on the top of the wall. Pulling with his elbows and arms, he hoists himself through the temporary hole in the roof. The tin slaps back down in place with a twang.

Badger looks at the roof of the unguarded jail cell. He climbs onto the bunk and reaches for the tin. He stands on the tips of his toes and raises the roof about a foot.

"Percy, come help," Badger says without looking at his friend. "If I can sneak out, I can go see if that bag of money is still in the Nevada Hotel."

"You can reach, Badger; just climb out," Percy says.

"I know I can, but it'll be easier if you give me a boost," Badger says.

"Okay," Percy replies, getting up. "You should go to Doc Bettis's, too, to see if Frank Newton is still there."

Percy stands on the bunk beside Badger. He cups his hands and leans down slightly. Badger puts one foot atop Percy's hands. They bounce together twice, and then Badger jumps as Percy lifts. Badger's head bangs into the tin roof as his elbows latch onto the top edge of the rock-and-concrete wall. The pudgy teen shimmies out the opening. Badger finds his balance and looks back down at his friend.

"Reach here, Percy, and I'll pull you out," Badger says.

"Even though we're innocent, Badger, it's against the law to escape from jail," Percy says. "I started today gettin' a crate of pickles ready to sell, and now I'm in jail. I'm not gonna make it worse. I'll stay here, thank you. If the sheriff comes back, I'll try to cover for you."

Badger looks at his friend once more and then reluctantly closes the tin roof. He climbs down the wall and scurries to the back of the jail. Badger looks around nervously. He has to find evidence that will clear his name. But if he gets caught, he'll be in even bigger trouble, just like Percy said. Badger shifts into the shadows but finds no comfort in the darkness.

BADGER SNEAKS BEHIND DOC BETTIS'S office. The building is perfectly square and has a pyramid roof. Badger looks into the first window and sees a desk and small library of leather-bound books. Badger slinks down the wall and peers through a corner of another window. Badger spots a bed in the middle of the room, and Frank Newton is in it. Frank, breathing slowly, appears to be asleep. His head is bandaged, and a blanket covers most of his body.

Badger sinks to the ground. He is as confused as a first-grader looking at his brother's algebra studies. He scratches his head and peers up at the starry sky. *If the man Percy and I saw on Cripmen Grade wasn't Frank Newton, who was he?* Badger wonders. The young cowboy shakes his head and searches his mind for an explanation.

As Badger stews deep in thought, the front door of the doctor's office gingerly opens and quietly closes. The same routine is repeated at the door leading into Frank's recovery room. A small candle is ignited, and a few rays of light escape through the window under which Badger is sitting. Badger hurries to his feet and peeks inside.

"This was not part of the deal, you moron," a woman's voice says. Badger sees Mrs. Dubois standing over the motionless Frank. She always seems to wear a fancy outfit, but they're all different. Today's hat is smaller than the one she wore in the stagecoach, and it is full of feathers. Badger would love to see what kind of bird made those feathers.

"I buried the two sacks, just like you told me to do. I can't explain what happened to the $1,200 I left for you," a man's voice replies.

Badger thinks the voice sounds like Frank's, but it is too muffled for him to be certain. Badger squints his eyes at the scene inside, but he still can't see Frank's face.

"It just didn't work as smooth as I had hoped," the man says.

Badger looks around the room but can't see who is speaking. *Maybe someone is standin' in the shadows,* Badger thinks.

"I want this mess fixed," Mrs. Dubois says, "and I want what we agreed on. If you can't find it, I can make life very miserable for you Mr.—" Mrs. Dubois abruptly stops speaking and looks straight at Badger. "We are being watched," she says as she walks to the window.

Badger drops below the sill and presses his body against the wall. He holds his breath to keep quiet. Badger hears urgent mumbling but can't make out any words. The light from the window flickers out, and Badger uses the darkness to escape. His trip to Doc Bettis's office leaves the young cowboy with more questions than answers. *Who was that hoity-toity lady talkin' to?* Badger wonders. *Who was the man at the top of Crippen Grade?*

Badger breathes in the cool night air. Despite being in the bottom of a canyon, Jarbidge is still high in the mountains. Badger's lungs burn from the short hike in the thin air. He takes several deep gasps to calm his breathing as he follows the gently sloped dirt road up to the Nevada Hotel's parlor window. Peeking through the window, Badger sees Johnny and three other men sitting around a green, felt-covered table. They slouch in their chairs and hold playing cards in their hands. Johnny clutches his cards clumsily. Each man has a pile of coins and bills in front of him. Through the thin walls, Badger hears their conversation.

"Do you think you'll get out of jail, Johnny?" one man asks. The man is clearly a miner. He wears a dirty brown hat, dirty brown shirt, and dirty brown pants. He has a long beard and squints like he has been in the dark underground for hours.

"I'm certain I will," Johnny replies, "one way or another."

All the players chuckle.

Johnny continues, "I know where the money is, and I'm pretty sure I can get the judge to pin the robbery on someone else."

28

"Who would look more guilty than you?" another man asks. This player looks like a poorer version of Johnny. He doesn't have the well-worn clothes of a laborer or the fine attire of an accomplished gambler. "After the bad run of luck you're havin' tonight, it's obvious you need the money."

"That is true," Johnny tells his new friends. "But this kid who's locked up with me looks as guilty as a person can be. His conscience must be botherin' him, though, because he and his pal brought the sheriff two-thirds of the stolen money. But the kid had to have some help robbin' the stage, because he's as dumb as a fence post. I don't think he's bright enough to plan something like this himself. And the scrawny boy with him doesn't have a thief's backbone."

Badger slides to the ground and angrily looks at the sky. *Dumb as a fence post; not bright enough,* Badger thinks. *I'll show that lyin' skunk tomorrow in court. I'll tell the judge Johnny Greene knows where the money is and that he is tryin' to pin the blame on me.* Badger slowly rises and then walks quickly down the street.

ABOUT HALFWAY BACK TO the jail, Badger sees the sheriff sauntering along. Sheriff Blakely is still chewing the last bite of his meal and has a white cloth napkin tucked into his shirt collar. Badger runs as quietly as he can, keeping to the shadows behind the buildings. As the sheriff reaches the jail's entrance, the older man stops and removes his left boot. He tips it upside down and jiggles out two small pebbles.

Badger breaks into a crouching sprint, knowing he has to be in the jail cell when the sheriff arrives or face a heap of trouble.

The sheriff shoves his stocking-clad foot back into the boot and leans heavily against the wall. He swallows hard and closes his eyes tightly. He inhales deeply and gently rubs his potbelly to ease his indigestion. The sheriff belches, pulls the napkin from his collar, and reaches for the door.

At the same time, Badger flings himself at the jail's six-foot-tall rock-and-mortar wall and scurries up it. He grabs the top edge of the wall just as his cowboy boots slip. Holding tightly, Badger dangles like a dead varmint slung over a fence. He pulls up with his arms and finds a toehold for one boot. Then he slips again, and his left boot falls to the ground. His stocking-covered toes find a crease in the rock, and Badger uses it to push himself to the wall's edge. Wheezing, the teen loses his balance and falls face-first onto the tin roof, shattering the night's quiet. His weight forces the panel inward, and with a *TWANG, THUMP, CRASH*, Badger plummets to the bunk.

Hearing the commotion, Sheriff Blakely rushes inside, his gun drawn. The sheriff blinks to adjust his eyes to the dark and looks through the cell door's steel bars. Percy sits uncomfortably in the corner of the cell, and Badger lies on the bunk where he landed.

"Well, shave my head and call me baldy. What's goin' on in here?" the sheriff barks.

Percy looks up with a tepid smile. "We're just sittin' here waitin' for dinner."

"You haven't been sneakin' out, have you?" the sheriff asks.

"We haven't," Badger says between deep breaths, "but Mr. Greene escaped."

The sheriff laughs. "Of course he's escaped. Every gambler knows about the weak roofs in jails. I'll let you in on a little secret. There's not enough gold in the mines up here to support all these businesses. If the saloons and hotels and stores are gonna survive, we gotta have more money comin' in than goin' out. Johnny

Greene has cash, and the more he loses in our town, the better off we'll be."

"Even if he's gamblin' with stolen payroll?" Badger asks.

"Now, boys, he's innocent until he goes in front of the justice of the peace—er, I mean, in front of me tomorrow."

"Well, I might have a surprise for you tomorrow," Badger says as he stares at the sheriff. "I think Mr. Greene is gonna place the blame on me. But I know something about him that'll surprise everyone."

"Johnny Greene wasn't carryin' a gun, Badger; you were. Johnny Greene wasn't guardin' the stage; you were. And Johnny Greene didn't stroll into my office with $1,200; you did. I still have a hunch Johnny had a hand in the robbery; he might even know where the rest of the money is. But knowin' what I know," the sheriff replies, "it'll take a miracle to clear your name, son."

"Expect a miracle, Sheriff."

Chapter Four

A MUFFLED CHORUS OF chatter fills the Jarbidge Commercial Club's main room. Jarbidge doesn't have a courthouse, so court is held in this building, which is usually unused during the day. Sheriff Blakely sits cross-armed at a table in front of the stage. Curtains hang open at either side of the platform. A painted scene used in the club's performances covers the area's back wall. A large desk and chair squat atop the stage, awaiting the justice of the peace. Johnny, Badger, and Percy sit at two tables, facing the stage.

Johnny leans over from his table, snickers at Badger, and says, "Are you glad I brought your boot back to you last night? It'd be unfortunate to walk to your day in court in your stockin' feet."

Badger forces a sarcastic smile onto his face and then turns to Percy and grimaces.

Sheriff Blakely pulls his watch from his vest pocket, looks at the time, and jumps to life. He grabs the hammer-shaped gavel and bangs it on the table like a carpenter at quitting time.

"All rise for the Honorable Thomas Blakely, Jarbidge's justice of the peace," Sheriff Blakely says with an authoritative tone to his voice.

The crowd rises and murmurs as Sheriff Blakely scoots out of his chair. He slips a black robe over his head, climbs up the stairs, walks across the stage, and sits down at the desk.

"You may be seated."

And with that, Sheriff Blakely becomes Justice of the Peace Blakely.

Justice of the Peace Blakely shuffles through his papers and looks at his notes.

"This is an evidentiary hearing, not a trial," Justice Blakely says. "I will simply review the evidence and determine whether there's enough to hold you for trial. Accordin' to the sheriff's report, Johnny Greene and Lawrence 'Badger' Thurston, you are charged with robbin' the Jarbidge mail stage. Percy Reed, you're charged with bein' an accessory to robbery.

"On Tuesday afternoon, Mr. Greene requested the stage stop so he could exit the stagecoach. While the stage was stopped, two shots were fired. Mr. Thurston was the only person in the group known to be carryin' a weapon, which was a shotgun that could shoot two shots. The stagecoach's horses stampeded, and Mr. Greene removed $1,800 in payroll from the stagecoach after the run away. Mr. Thurston and Mr. Reed recovered and returned two-thirds of the money. One-third of the money, presumably Mr. Greene's share, has not been recovered yet. Lawrence 'Badger' Thurston, Percy Reed, and Johnny Greene, do you plead guilty or not guilty?"

"Not guilty," the three respond in chorus.

"All right, Mr. Thurston, let's start with you," Justice Blakely says. "What can you say in your defense?"

"First, I'd never met Mr. Greene before he got on the stagecoach, and I would never work with a thievin' gambler. Second, I am certain Mr. Greene stole the money," Badger says loudly. Badger looks as mad as a wet cat as he speaks.

"Now, Mr. Thurston, you can't just make accusations. You need proof."

"I have proof," Badger responds. "Last night, Mr. Greene, a man I hadn't met before he stepped onto the stage, escaped from jail, and I followed him. At the Nevada Hotel, I overheard him tell the other gamblers that he was gonna frame me."

"I did not," Johnny says with an arrogant grin.

"Wait your turn, Mr. Greene," Justice Blakely says. "You can defend yourself next. And Mr. Thurston, you might wanna explain why *you* escaped from my jail last night."

"I just followed Mr. Greene," Badger says forcefully while pointing a finger at Johnny. Badger pauses for dramatic effect, still pointing at Johnny. "I had my suspicions about him all along. He was the one who asked the stage to stop at the top of Crippen Grade. My gun was unloaded, and the shots came from behind me."

"Wait, wait, wait," Justice Blakely interrupts. "Why was your gun unloaded?"

"Frank Newton didn't give me any ammunition," Badger says matter-of-factly.

"I find that very hard to believe, Mr. Thurston," Justice Blakely replies. "Why bother hirin' a guard only to arm him with an empty shotgun?"

35

"I was just supposed to be an actor," Badger says hesitantly as he hears how silly his own words sound.

Justice Blakely guffaws and says, "You may continue."

"As I was sayin', the shots came from behind me. Mr. Greene would have had a chance to pull a hidden pistol and fire the shots that scared the stagecoach's horses. It is true that me and Percy recovered some of the stolen money, but a rider brought the rest of it to the Nevada Hotel. Mr. Greene knew about the jail's flimsy roof, and he had enough time to hide the missin' third of the money at the Nevada Hotel."

The justice of the peace nods his head. He looks like he's about to laugh. As he writes down a few notes, Badger collects his thoughts.

"Do you have anything else to say for yourself?" Justice Blakely asks.

"I think Frank Newton is in on it," Badger says.

Justice Blakely chuckles twice, breaking into Badger's train of thought. "You expect me to believe Frank Newton stole from the very stagecoach he was drivin', the stagecoach his father owns? I don't believe that for a second. And smackin' his head on a branch that knocks him silly, was that part of the plan?"

"But I was knocked out, too," Badger pleads. "I took the same fall Frank Newton did."

"But you're awake now, and he's still knocked out at Doc Bettis's office and not here to defend himself," Justice Blakely sings to Badger. "And that still doesn't answer why Frank Newton would wanna rob his family's stagecoach."

Badger stands silently as he listens to the justice of the peace. Badger's anger and embarrassment turn his face as red as a rotten tomato. *Why won't anyone believe me?* Badger wonders. *I think my story is very believable.*

"Do you have any other outrageous claims to make?" Justice Blakely asks. "Would you like to blame Mrs. Dubois while you're at it? She was on the stagecoach, too, and you have yet to accuse her."

"I'm innocent," Badger pleads. "Can't you see I'm innocent?"

"Do you have any more evidence to present?" Justice Blakely asks as he looks down his nose at Badger.

Badger hangs his head as his shoulders slump. "I have nothin' more to say," he says in a small voice.

Badger plops down in his seat like a boxer after the tenth round as the justice shuffles through his notes again. The courtroom buzzes quietly as the gallery's audience members whisper among themselves.

"Okay, Mr. Greene, what do you have to say for yourself?" Justice Blakely asks.

"Well, your honor, I have been accused of robbing the stage, but let us examine the evidence," Johnny says.

Badger winces as he realizes he never called Justice Blakely "your honor."

"First, I have never been to Jarbidge before," Johnny continues. "So I neither knew of nor chose the Crippen Grade stopping spot; Frank Newton did. Furthermore, Frank Newton's coffee, not mine, hastened my request to stop at that spot—"

"Not you, too," Justice Blakely interrupts. "Why would Frank Newton rob his family's stagecoach? He has no motive, and you, Mr. Greene, have no alibi."

"I will get straight to my point, your honor. I agree with Mr. Thurston that we were not working together. In fact, I have a train stub that proves I was in Denver at the beginning of the week. So the culprit could only be one of us, either Mr. Thurston or me, who committed the crime. Your honor, would you agree that the person who fired the shot that spooked the horses perpetrated the crime?"

"That seems reasonable," Justice Blakely says. "Please continue, Mr. Greene."

"Well, sir, I do not own a gun," Johnny says with a lopsided smile.

Badger scratches his head, and a puzzled look slowly plasters itself on his face.

"In fact, your honor, I cannot even fire a gun."

"That seems improbable, Mr. Greene. Would you care to explain?"

"Certainly. When I was a child, I hid beneath my father's buckboard wagon on several occasions. One time when I was hiding there, the horses spooked and the wheels rolled over both my hands," Johnny says.

The gambler pauses, pulls off his black gloves, and raises his two mangled hands.

"Both of my hands were crushed, and most of the joints in my hands do not work," Johnny continues. "I cannot button a shirt or vest. I cannot wear a tie—"

"And you can't fire a gun," Justice Blakely interrupts.

"I am unable to do most respectable work. I can use my hands to hold cards," Johnny says, positioning his hands to show how. "And I can use my brain to earn a little bit of money. If I were engaged in any other respectable profession, I probably would not be on trial here today."

"Johnny Greene, based on the evidence you have presented here today, you are free to go," Sheriff Blakely says. "And if you've gambled away all your money, I would recommend movin' on to the next town. Is forty-eight hours long enough for you to pack up and leave?"

38

"I'll be gone in twenty-four, your honor," Johnny says with a smirk.

Since Johnny cleared his name, Badger and Percy are the only suspects remaining. Badger shakes his head and stands up.

"Your honor," Badger says quickly, "Percy Reed didn't have anything to do with this. He was at his parents' store in Three Creek and couldn't have been on Crippen Grade. I'm sure you could ask anyone who was at the store Tuesday. Percy didn't even know I had hired on with the stagecoach until your rider came to his parent's store. He is only guilty of bein' a good friend and tryin' to help me out."

"Badger, what are you doin'?" Percy asks quietly.

"I can't prove I'm innocent if we're both in jail," Badger whispers. "If you're out, you can look for clues to get me out."

The justice of the peace looks down at Badger and Percy. He shakes his head. "I have proof Mr. Reed walked through the front door of my—er, Sheriff Blakely's jail with the recovered money. But nothin' else links him to the robbery. Percy Reed, you will not be held for trial."

Percy wipes his hand across his forehead, lets out a breath, and slouches in his chair.

"But you did mislead me, er, I mean, Sheriff Blakely about Mr. Thurston escapin' from jail last night. That's gonna cost you. You're free to go—tomorrow."

"But, your honor—" Badger says.

"But nothin'," Justice Blakely interrupts, raising his voice. "Mr. Thurston, your trial will begin Tuesday when the circuit judge comes through here. You'll remain in the Jarbidge Jail, and we'll try to scrounge up a lawyer for you in the meantime. Until then, no funny business."

The justice slams his hammer-shaped gavel on the table. With that, the hearing is over.

PERCY TOSSES A SMALL rock into the air and catches it. He tosses it up and catches it again. He tosses it and catches it. Tosses it, catches it. Toss. Catch. Toss. Catch.

"Stop it!" Badger says, not angrily but annoyed. "I'm havin' a hard enough time not goin' crazy, Percy. I'm tryin' to think up a plan to get out of here."

"I'm not worried," Percy says. "I get out in the mornin'."

"What about me?" Badger raises his voice. He jumps out of the bunk he is resting on while Percy leans back on his wooden bunk. Badger rubs his eyes and nose and calms his voice. "I could go to prison, and I'm the only suspect."

"Are you sure you didn't do it?" Percy asks. "It seems like all the evidence points to you."

"Not you, too," Badger says, shaking his head.

"Badger, I still believe you—for no other reason except you're my best friend. But we need to come up with an alibi for you or another suspect."

Badger wipes a dribble of sweat off his forehead. The cell is cool, but Badger is sweating like a steam-engine fireman. He paces the cell to let off some nervous energy. He takes off his hat and scratches the top of his head.

Percy looks up at Badger. "What about Frank Newton?"

"What about him? You heard the judge," Badger says.

"Yeah, but both you and Mr. Greene seem to think he was involved," Percy says as he sits up and leans forward on his bunk.

"You know, that rider we followed down the hill with the money looked just like Frank Newton," Badger says. "But how could Frank be the rider while bein' laid up at Doc Bettis's?"

"You know him better than I do," Percy says. "What makes you think it was Frank?"

"Who else do you know who wears all gray?" Badger asks. "Gray hat, gray vest, gray pants—the rider wore all gray. Frank's the only person I know who's weird like that for gray."

"Maybe he's not hurt," Percy says as he stares at his pebble. "Maybe Frank's just pretendin' to be hurt so he can stay at Doc Bettis's place and not have to answer any questions."

"I gotta get back down to Doc Bettis's and see if I can get inside," Badger says. "I need to see for myself how banged up Frank Newton really is."

"How are you gonna get out?" Percy asks.

"I have a plan, but I need your help," Badger says, looking directly at Percy.

Percy fidgets uncomfortably and looks around the cell. "Now, Badger," he says forcefully, "I have to spend tonight in jail because you snuck out last night. Why should I risk more jail time for one of your schemes?"

Badger shrugs his shoulders and puts his hands in his pockets. He steps closer to Percy and exhales sharply. "If we do this right, you'll be out of jail and safely on your way home, and they'll just let me go."

Percy pushes back his hat and scratches his head. "I bet I'm not gonna like your plan. I never like plans of yours that involve me. But I'm curious, so let's hear it."

"Well, Justice Blakely said you have to stay in jail until tomorrow. At midnight tonight, it will be tomorrow, and you can go, just like Justice Blakely said."

"But who's gonna come let me out?" Percy asks.

"Nobody, Percy, that's the plan," Badger says. The young cowboy is very animated as he explains the rest of his idea. He raises his arms and waves his hands wildly.

Percy nods and says very little. He leans closer as he listens to Badger's scheme like an edgy horse when the grass rustles.

"Whattaya think?" Badger asks.

"Great plan," Percy says with a smile, "but I don't think it'll work."

"Why do you always say that?" Badger asks. "You never like my plans."

"Why do you always want me to fire a warnin' shot?" Percy replies. "I still don't have a gun. I'm still not a gunslinger. And your last big plan almost got you shot by a cattle rustler. I have a feelin' I'd be the target this time."

"Not all my plans are bad," Badger says. "We each made $30 on the cattle drive. And another time, we had fun saddlin' up and ridin' Mr. Gaar's steer. That was a great plan."

"No, it wasn't! Your warnin' shot that time was from a slingshot, and it made the steer buck. I got my foot caught in a stirrup, and that steer kicked me in the mouth. My tooth is still loose!" Percy says as he reaches two fingers into his mouth and wiggles a front tooth. "You had fun laughin' at me, but that doesn't mean it was a 'great plan.' I'm not interested in any of your plans that includes a warnin' shot."

"Okay, okay," Badger says, "everything but the warnin' shot."

"I still don't know, Badger. Why should I risk goin' back to jail by sneakin' out?" Percy asks.

Badger takes a deep breath to calm down and think. He tucks his pointer finger inside his shirt and digs into his belly button. He pulls out a small glob of lint and carefully examines it. He sniffs it, recoils with disgust, and then quickly flicks the lint ball across the jail cell. With his belly button clean, he turns his attention back to Percy.

"I already told you, Percy," Badger says as calmly as he can. "We'll wait till midnight so you'll be legal. Besides, everybody'll think it's me who's escaped. And Percy, this might be the only chance I have. I could be sent to prison for years if I can't get this mess settled."

Percy grimaces as he avoids eye contact with Badger. He looks at the ceiling and nervously chuckles. "I'm crazy to keep helpin' you, but I'll do what I can."

"Thanks, Percy. I owe you," Badger says with a relieved smile.

"Boy, isn't that the truth! You owe me big," Percy says. "Hey, maybe you could teach me to dance. Bertha Jo Stillwell has been makin' googly eyes at me whenever she comes into the store."

"Maybe I'll help you with that load of pickles instead," Badger says as he rolls his eyes. "Let's get started."

Badger quickly unbuttons his red plaid shirt and strips it off his back. Percy works more methodically, slowly taking his blue shirt off. The two exchange shirts. Badger squeezes into Percy's as Percy pulls on Badger's. Badger hands his brown hat to Percy, and Percy gives his gray hat to Badger.

"What do you think, Percy?" Badger asks. "Do I look like you?"

"As long as it's dark and no one looks too closely," Percy replies. "Do I look like you?"

"You look like me if I've been eatin' jail food for about a month. My shirt's huge on you, Percy."

"You don't think this'll work?" Percy asks.

"No, no," Badger says. "Just don't let anyone get too close to you. Remember, once you get your horse, go up Jack Creek and through Robinson Hole over to the Gaar Place. If Old Man Gaar's there, he'll help you. He still has an account at your parent's store, doesn't he? If he's not home, follow the creek down and over to your parents' store. You need to find someone to say you're you and not me."

Percy checks the clock on the wall of the sheriff's office. The little hand is just past the twelve, and the big hand rests on the two. He takes a deep breath and looks up at the flimsy tin roof.

"Well, here goes," Percy says. "But I'm givin' up once the shootin' starts."

"You'll be fine, and there won't be any shootin'," Badger says as he cups his hands to give Percy a boost. "Just get your horse from the livery and ride. I'll give you about an hour, and then I'll yell that I've escaped. I'll keep my back to the door, so the sheriff sees only your shirt and hat. Stay on a trail, so the sheriff's posse can track you. If the men lose your trail, they'll come back and find me missin', too, and then they'll be ready to measure me for permanent shackles. But if they catch you—"

"I know," Percy says, "then I'll be the one bein' measured for shackles."

Percy steps into Badger's hands. They bounce twice, and then Percy jumps up like a lop-eared jackrabbit and shimmies out through the tin roof. Badger settles back down onto his bunk and searches for an hour of restless sleep.

BADGER TOSSES AND TURNS in the dark cell. He can't see that morning is dawning, but he can hear the town slowly waking up. Badger hears a rooster crow in the distance. Doors bang open and shut, and a few wagons and people stroll down the dusty street. Badger shivers and searches for a soft spot on his hard bunk. As the teen blinks the sleep from his eyes, the jail door slowly inches open, and a woman walks in.

"Hello, sonny," the woman says as she peers through the cell door. "My husband, the sheriff, is out of town chasin' a fugitive. He told me to release you this mornin', so you're free to go."

"Thank you, ma'am," Badger says. "What's your name?"

"Why do you wanna know my name?"

"A lot of people have been escapin' from the jail lately. If anyone asks, I want proof I was released," Badger says politely.

"My name is June Blakely," she replies. Mrs. Blakely looks like a female version of Sheriff Blakely. She has gray hair and a neatly pressed but well-worn green plaid dress. "You don't have anything to worry about, sonny. Everyone who would notice is followin' the thief who escaped last night."

Badger sighs in relief and then quickly coughs to hide his relief. Mrs. Blakely jiggles a key into the lock, and the cell door swings open. Badger nods and tips his hat to Mrs. Blakely before stepping outside. He pauses in the sunshine for a moment and enjoys the warmth. Badger guesses he has until nightfall to find the evidence he needs. He looks up the narrow, dusty street and then back down it. He doesn't know what he is looking for. He lifts Percy's hat with a finger and scratches his head. *Mr. Greene,* Badger thinks, *he'll have some answers.*

Chapter Five

THE PARLOR OF THE Nevada Hotel is dark and smoky. A little stove crackles and pops as the wood burns and warms the small, quiet room. Badger sits down in a velvet chair to wait for Johnny. The young cowboy hears voices and activities going on in the tiny hotel's ten other rooms. Badger's stomach rumbles as he smells breakfast cooking down the hall. Badger resists his belly's urgings to go find food. He can't risk being seen out of jail. He twists to the left and then to the right. He fidgets with Percy's tight shirt. Badger stands up and looks out the window. He sits back down and adjusts Percy's shirt again. Weary of waiting, he stands up to leave. As Badger walks to the door, Johnny finally enters the parlor, carrying his coat and a small bag.

"Well, well, well," Johnny says, "I heard you had escaped, Badger, but I thought you were long gone."

"You can't believe every word you hear," Badger says, "and things aren't always as they seem."

Johnny places his bag on the floor and sits in the chair Badger had occupied moments before. He removes his hat and sets it neatly beneath the chair. "Have you come to accuse me of other crimes?" Johnny asks. "I think I made it pretty clear I wasn't involved."

"I don't know what to believe anymore," Badger says with an impolite sneer. "I just know I didn't rob the stagecoach, and I'm tryin' to clear my name."

"I've heard a few stories around town, and I know you didn't do it," Johnny says with an annoying grin.

"Because I'm not smart enough," Badger asks, "or because you were in on the robbery?"

"I don't have an opinion on your intelligence, Badger, but your manners leave something to be desired," Johnny says as he leans back in the chair and crosses his legs. "I think I know who did it, but I am disinclined to help someone who even now throws accusations at me."

Badger is silent. Johnny might be the only one who can help him, and now Badger is on his wrong side.

"I'm sorry, Mr. Greene," Badger says, "but I'm desperate for answers."

"Well, I don't have all the answers, and I still don't wanna help you," Johnny says as he trains a steely glare at Badger. "But, look, one of the guys I was playin' cards with the other night said someone lookin' like Frank Newton had come through the hotel's front door only to walk straight out its back door. But I'm not sayin' another word."

Badger's eyes dance as Johnny speaks. *Either Frank has an identical twin, or Frank is fakin' his injuries,* Badger thinks. *And it seems Frank was actin' to frame both me and Johnny. That's why he gave me a gun but no bullets.* Badger is silent for a minute because he wants Johnny to volunteer more information.

"Is that all you know?" Badger finally asks. "Is there something you're not tellin' me?"

"That's all I'm tellin'," Johnny says with a devious smile. "I've already talked too much. I still don't wanna help you."

"Well, you have helped me, and I thank you," Badger says as he steps toward the door.

"Good luck, Badger," Johnny says. "You'll need it if the rest of my guesses are right."

Badger pauses and looks back at Johnny. He opens his mouth to speak but instead quietly turns and walks out the door.

AS BADGER APPROACHES Doc Bettis's office, he sees a silky, black feather lying on the ground. Badger has been told that sticking a feather in your hat is good luck, so he settles the silky feather under Percy's hatband. He tucks in Percy's too-small shirt and steps to the front door.

Badger knocks twice and waits. He knocks twice more and waits again. Growing impatient, he tries the doorknob. It's unlocked, so the teen gingerly steps inside. Badger closes the door behind him and glides over to the room's only interior door. He cracks it open and peeks inside. Frank is stretched out on a bed; his head is bandaged. For a second, Frank looks like he has one eye open. Badger sneaks inside like a cat burglar and closes the door.

"Frank, can you hear me?" Badger whispers as he stands over the stagecoach driver. "Frank? Frank!"

Frank's smooth skin barely moves as he breathes slowly. Badger chews on his bottom lip as he looks at Frank. Then Badger's eyes light up. He pulls the feather out of Percy's hatband and lightly brushes it along Frank's bird-like nose. The stage driver grins for a moment. Badger touches the feather to Frank's chin, and his boss's hand swats it away. But Frank's eyes are still closed. Badger twirls the feather in Frank's ear, and Frank turns his head away. Badger tickles the feather down Frank's neck. Suddenly, Frank sits bolt upright and snatches the feather away.

"Stop ticklin' me, you idiot!" he snarls.

"I thought you were hurt," Badger says sourly.

"I, uh, um ... I was, er, I mean, I am," Frank says nervously.

"What are you hidin', Frank?" Badger asks directly.

"I'm not hidin' anything," Frank says defensively. "I hit my head when the horses stampeded, and I can't remember the past three days."

"If you can't remember anything, how do you know three days have past?"

"I ... uh ... er ... well, you see ... I was told about it?" Frank suggests weakly. He pauses with a hopeful glint in his eyes.

"I'm not buyin' it, Frank," Badger says, "and I'm lookin' for answers."

"Well, I'm not talkin'," Frank says, mashing his lips together. "Besides, everyone thinks I'm hurt. I'll just go back to sleep."

"Oh no, you won't!" Badger yells angrily. "I'll tell everyone. I wasn't the only person to see you run into the Nevada Hotel with the money."

"Nobody'll believe you. Besides, the money isn't in the Nevada Hotel. I ran through the hotel and left my bag at a purple house up the street," Frank says with a laugh. "And really, Badger, I don't have any money. Some moron took the two-thirds I buried up on the grade and turned it in to the sheriff, so my partner took my $600. She's mad at me, and I'm scared of 'er."

"Her?" Badger exclaims. "Who is she? Who has the money?"

50

"She?" Franks asks. "I … uh … er … well, I didn't say 'she.' I said 'he.' My uh … partner is just some guy you wouldn't know."

A grin creeps across Badger's face. *I have my first real clue! Frank Newton was in on the heist, and he conspired with a woman. The only problem is Frank doesn't have the stolen payroll.*

"Thanks, Frank. You've been a real help. Just go on back to sleep—if you can."

"Badger, I'll give you the same advice my partner gave me. 'Dead men don't talk.' Prison doesn't seem so bad compared to bein' shot dead."

Badger shudders. *One thousand eight hundred dollars is a lot of money,* he thinks, *so whoever stole it would be that ruthless.*

Badger walks to the door, looks over his shoulder at Frank, and sighs. Then he exits the doctor's office and cautiously looks up and down the street. His thoughts find their way back to Mrs. Dubois and the conversation he overheard two days ago in this very office.

But why would she steal the payroll? he wonders. *She's rich.* Badger's mind races around in search of an explanation, but Badger can't figure out why Mrs. Dubois would want to steal the money that was supposed to pay her family's mine workers. Badger has more questions he wants answers to, but now he is scared and doesn't know where to go.

AS BADGER WANDERS DOWN the street, he spots the livery stables, and an idea creeps into his brain. He will get a horse. He'll ride north until he reaches Canada. He'll start a new life in a new country where no one knows who he is and what he has done. But Badger knows Percy will end up in jail if he's gone when the sheriff gets back. Badger shakes his head as he searches for another solution.

As Badger approaches the livery, he hears the *CLANG, CLANG, CLANG* of a steel hammer striking a steel horseshoe on a steel anvil. The rhythmic racket continues as Badger enters the stables. He sees a man working near a big sorrel horse. The muscular man strikes a steel horseshoe once more and then uses pincers to carry the red-hot shoe to the horse. The horse looks slightly overworked and slightly underfed.

His hair is a bit matted, and he shows the effects of having eaten the area's stale late-fall feed.

The man's worn-out body looks older than his bright eyes suggest. His overalls are tattered and dirty, and sweat drips off his dirty blond hair. His beard is long, and he wears a kerchief tied tightly around his neck.

The man steps close to the horse's front, left hoof and gently puts his hand on the creature's neck. With the hot shoe held tightly with the pincer in his right hand, he leans down and tugs on the horse's fetlock at the back of his hoof.

"Gimme your foot, you rotgut son of a mule!" the man yells at the horse.

The sorrel slowly lifts his hoof. The man places the shoe beneath it and pulls a small, square nail from a rolled cuff in the leg of his overalls. The man hammers the nail through a small hole in the horseshoe into the horse's hard hoof. The nail piercing the hoof hurts the horse just about as much as it would hurt a boy to get his toenails trimmed. After about three strikes, though, the horse flinches.

"Hold still, you mangy, dad-burned, skunk-eatin', speckled pony!" the man bellows.

The horse sighs and pins his ears back. The man strikes the nail twice more, and the nail emerges from the top of the horse's hoof like a snake crawling out of a ground-squirrel hole. The man uses his hammer to bend the sharp nail back down against the hoof. He grabs another nail and repeats the procedure. As he strikes the third nail, the horse swats at a fly with his tail.

"Stand still, you egg-suckin' rat fink!" the man shouts.

The horse leans all his weight on the man. The horse is used to standing on four legs, and after a short period, the lazy beast uses the man as his fourth leg. The farrier can't hold up the horse's weight. So he steps out from under the sorrel, and the horse drops his front hoof to the ground.

"You lily-livered, flea-bitten, old nag!" the man hollers.

He takes a deep breath and stands up straight. He arches his back to ease the pain of his hard work. After all this, he finally notices Badger.

"Well, hello there, sonny," the man says. "My name is Gene Starlin'. If it's a horse you're lookin' for, then have I got a deal for you."

Badger takes a moment to collect his thoughts and then says, "Well, I'm Badger, and I need a horse in the worst way."

"Are you lookin' to rent or buy?" Gene asks.

"Well, I guess I'm lookin' to borrow," Badger says as he stares at the ground and kicks a pebble. "I don't really have any money."

"Jumpin' Jehoshaphat!" Gene exclaims with a laugh. "You just want me to give you a horse?"

"Well, I'm kind of in a tough spot. I came over here workin' on the stagecoach that was robbed. I didn't get paid, and now I'm stuck here."

"You're not the boy who escaped from jail last night, are you?" Gene asks.

"Mrs. Blakely released me from the jail this mornin'. I do have a court date comin' up though. I'm just out tryin' to clear my name."

"I heard the guy ridin' shotgun robbed the stage. He was the only one with a gun," Gene says.

Badger winces. "I heard the guy ridin' shotgun heard two shots ring out behind him. And Mr. Greene couldn't have fired 'em," Badger says, hoping to drop a new fish in the gossip pond.

"Well, if Johnny Greene didn't do it, who else could've? Who else was back there?"

Badger shrugs his shoulders. "Mrs. Dubois was the only other passenger. I'm not sure who else it could be."

"Madeline Dubois, huh?" Gene says. "You wanna hear a rumor about her?"

"Sure," Badger says, "if you think it'll help."

"Well, word around town is Mrs. Dubois is leavin' her husband. That's just a rumor, though, and I don't like spreadin' rumors."

"Um ... so?" Badger asks, bewildered.

"Well, if she leaves Mr. Dubois, she doesn't get a penny. And if Mrs. Dubois doesn't get a penny, she might wanna acquire some cash of her own."

"You mean she might wanna steal some money?" Badger asks.

"I'm not *sayin'* she *might* wanna; I'm *implyin'* she *would* wanna," Gene says, rolling his eyes.

Badger scratches his head, looking confused. *I'm not quite sure what Mr. Starlin' is really tellin' me, and I'm not sure the rumor's true.*

"That still doesn't make any sense," Badger says.

"And you still don't have any money," Gene says as his eyes dance with laughter. "You're not goin' anywhere on horseback, so you might wanna look into all your leads."

Badger nods his head as Gene reaches down to lift the horse's front, left hoof. Gene taps more nails into the holes in the shoe, and Badger walks slowly away.

"Stand still, you sewer-swillin', cross-eyed, lop-eared burro!" Gene shouts.

Badger now has to do the one thing he is scared to do—talk to Mrs. Dubois.

Chapter Six

BADGER WALKS LIKE A condemned man approaching the gallows as he plods along Jarbidge's main street. He trudges up to the Dubois place. It's a shack like all the other residences in Jarbidge, but this shack is much more stately than the rest. Its front door is black, and its siding boards have been painted purple. The roof's shingles are uniform and stained black. Its porch holds a fancy, white bench. Badger is not impressed; because no matter how fancy the shack is, it is still just a shack.

Badger timidly climbs the stair to the front porch. He looks at the wall and wishes it had a window he could peek through to find more clues. He approaches the door and raps its knocker three times. Badger scratches his belly as he waits.

"I should have a servant to answer the door," a woman's voice snarls from inside.

The door swings open, and Mrs. Dubois emerges. She isn't wearing a hat, and her hair is matted down where a hat would usually be. Her fancy dress looks like an old, deflated balloon since she isn't wearing all the hoops and foofy frills she usually does. *She looks like she just woke up from a nap*, Badger thinks.

"What do you want?" Mrs. Dubois snaps.

"I ... uh ... er ... well," Badger blathers.

"Well, say it before I slam the door."

"Did you rob the stagecoach?" Badger blurts out. He slaps his forehead as he realizes how straightforward and rude his question is.

"How dare you insult me in front of my own home!" Mrs. Dubois hisses.

"Is that a yes?" Badger asks. "I just wanna know why you need the money. You're a rich woman—at least, your husband's rich."

"Enough of your baseless insinuation!" Mrs. Dubois yells.

Badger grins nervously. "It's just ... there's a rumor around town that you might've had a hand in the robbery. I'm tryin'—"

Badger clams up as Mrs. Dubois pulls a small pistol from between the pleats in her dress.

"I don't like the way you talk," Mrs. Dubois says in a measured tone. "This kind of talk could get a boy hurt—or even killed. You're out of jail. Why don't you just leave?"

Badger tries to speak, but the tiny gun's barrel makes him choke on his words. *Now is not a good time to lose your head*, Badger silently tells himself. *Calm down. Think ... think ... think.*

"You wouldn't shoot me," Badger says slyly. "What if you miss? I could get away and ..." Badger pauses, hoping Mrs. Dubois will interrupt him.

"My pistol has two shots," Mrs. Dubois says. "If I miss with the first, I will indubitably hit you with the second, you little twerp."

"Two shots in your little pistol," Badger says. "That's all I needed to hear. I'll take your suggestion and leave. Please forgive my, ah, how did you say— insolence."

Badger spins on his boot heel and walks briskly away, resisting several urges to look over his shoulder. *BANG!* The sound of Mrs. Dubois slamming her door rockets Badger's heart into his throat and sizzles his nerves, and the young cowboy takes off like a snake-bitten antelope.

BADGER STANDS IN FRONT of the Jarbidge Jail, deep in thought. He believes he has the critical piece of evidence he needs to clear his name. His only concern now is staying alive until the sheriff returns. The safest place in Jarbidge is in the jail's cell, but Badger is too tired to break in through the roof.

I've spent the past two days tryin' to get out of jail, he thinks. *Now when I want back in, I can't manage it.*

Badger steps inside the small, dimly lit sheriff's office. He drops into the chair behind the desk and rubs the bridge of his nose. As Badger looks at the cell longingly, he notices it isn't closed tightly. Badger pushes out of his seat, trudges over, and tugs on the cell's bars. The door swings open, and the corners of Badger's mouth creep toward both his ears. He steps into the cell and pulls the steel door shut behind him. Badger checks the latch; it's still unlocked.

As Badger tries to relax on the hard bunk, the jail's exterior door opens slightly, sending a beam of light across the sheriff's office. The barrel of a shotgun sticks through the doorway, and Badger shudders like an antsy rattlesnake. Badger quickly scans the cell, shimmies into a shadow, and crouches near the floor. Badger feels himself trembling as the gun wielder moves slowly inside. Badger sees a woman's hand gripping the gun, then a frilly lace cuff, and then a whole sleeve. Instantly, the cell door flings open and the barrel of the gun is aimed directly at Badger. Badger shrieks like a schoolgirl finding a jumping frog in her desk. He closes his eyes, expecting the worst.

"Who are you, and what do you want?" an older woman's voice yells.

Badger pries open one eye and spots June Blakely—not Madeline Dubois. She's trembling, and her finger is perilously close to squeezing the trigger.

"It's me, Badger Thurston," he cries. "I'm turnin' myself in."

Mrs. Blakely lowers the barrel of the rifle.

"Who ... what are you ... I don't understand," Mrs. Blakely replies.

"I'm turnin' myself in," Badger says again. "But I think I can prove I'm innocent."

Mrs. Blakely looks carefully at Badger. "Aren't you that Reed boy I turned loose this mornin'?"

"No, ma'am," Badger says confidently. *I am the boy you turned loose,* Badger thinks, *just not "that Reed boy."*

"You look just like him," Mrs. Blakely says.

"We look a lot alike. But I escaped, and I'm turnin' myself in."

"Well, all you boys look the same to me," Mrs. Blakely says. "You boys could at least wear different clothes to help an old lady out."

"Sorry, ma'am," Badger says as he tugs on Percy's too-tight shirt. "Percy and I have the same tailor."

60

"Well, I'll leave you be," Mrs. Blakely says as she pulls the door closed.

"Uh, Mrs. Blakely," Badger says, "could you please lock the cell door?"

"Sure, sonny. Sure."

"And the outside door, too?" Badger asks.

"That lock's broken," Mrs. Blakely says. "But I'll lock your cell."

Mrs. Blakely fumbles with a large ring of keys, locks the cell door, and leaves. Badger hides in the darkness as best he can and hopes the sheriff gets back soon—before Madeline Dubois comes for him.

PERCY GLANCES OVER HIS shoulder at six horses and their riders. In the past hour, the posse has gained about half a mile on him. Percy looks in front of him and sees the Gaar place about a mile ahead. Smoke climbs lazily from the cabin's chimney, so Percy knows someone is home.

Percy's white horse is covered with sweat and dust from the trail. Percy urges him to run faster. Snowball breaks into the slow lope of a worn-out horse. Percy feels like he is riding a rocking horse—swinging back and forth but not really moving. Percy's father would scold him if he knew how hard he was riding Snowball.

Percy takes a deep breath and looks back again at the sheriff's small band. The young cowboy is within a half-mile of the Gaar place now, but the menacing cloud of dust behind him is creeping closer and closer. He urges Snowball forward once more with a gentle kick to his belly. The weary horse leaps ahead with the encouragement but quickly slows again.

As Percy throws his chin over his shoulder to peer back at his pursuers, the exhausted Snowball stumbles. The motion sends Percy sailing over the beast's head to flop like a gunnysack full of rotten onions on the hard dirt.

Worn out from the ride and hurting from the fall, Percy lies where he landed. He looks at Snowball and frowns. Snowball's knees are locked, and his legs are splayed outward. His whole body shakes as he gasps for air. Percy knows his horse won't take another step. If Percy gets caught, though, he'll have to ride all the way back to Jarbidge in handcuffs. Not only would that be uncomfortable for Percy, it might kill Snowball.

With that urgent thought, Percy pulls his tired body from the ground. Percy's first three steps are labored. He feels like he has rocks tied to his boots. But Percy's feet start to churn as the trail heads downhill into the valley that holds the Gaar place. He has less than a

quarter-mile left to go, but the posse is quickly closing in. Suddenly, his right boot's toe catches on a rock, and Percy goes down with a grunt. Stretched belly-first in the dirt, Percy takes two deep breaths, remembers his mission, and clambers to his feet.

"Mr. Gaar!" Percy yells as he runs. "Mr. Gaar, help!"

Percy's voice falls on an empty trail. He runs faster as his legs and lungs burn.

"Help, Mr. Gaar!" Percy shouts in panic. "Mr. Gaar!"

A man rushes through the front door of the solitary cabin nestled in the steep-sided valley. He is pulling on a tattered coat and has bits of bread and bacon grease in his beard. He snatches up a rifle and steps off his front porch before walking past a small barn and striding through the gate in his three-pole fence.

Percy slows to a walk, and the man runs the distance between them. The posse is fifty yards away.

"Mr. Gaar," Percy pleads between gasps. "Help me. They're after me."

"Percy Reed, is that you?" Mr. Gaar asks. "What are you doin' up here?"

The sheriff and five other riders stop their horses near the pair. A cloud of dust floats past, covering everyone with a thin coat of trail grime. Percy coughs and puts his hands on his knees.

"What's goin' on here, Sheriff?" Mr. Gaar asks.

"John, that boy is an escaped prisoner," Sheriff Blakely says. "I intend to take him back to Jarbidge."

"Now, Tom, I know you're the judge in Jarbidge, but this is my place, and I'm judge here. You bein' sheriff and justice of the peace ended about twenty miles back at Jarbidge's city limits," Mr. Gaar says grimly. "Before I turn over Percy, you need to make your case to me."

"Percy!" Sheriff Blakely exclaims. "I'm after Badger Thurston."

"Well, I'm not Badger," Percy says. "I spent my night and left peacefully. That was my sentence, wasn't it? One more night."

The sheriff groans, and a bewildered look creeps across his face. "I don't understand," Sheriff Blakely says. "You were in the jail when I left. How are you here? And where is Badger?"

"Badger never left Jarbidge. You've been followin' Badger's shirt and hat, but it's me, Percy Reed, wearin' 'em."

Sheriff Blakely tilts his head to the right and scratches his ear. He looks at Percy and asks, "Why are you wearin' Badger's hat and shirt?"

"Okay, I'll tell you the whole truth," Percy says. "I'm a diversion. Badger needed a few more hours to prove he didn't rob the stagecoach. So we traded clothes so you would think I was Badger. But it *was* after midnight when I left."

"So, technically, it was tomorrow—er, today, like I ordered," Sheriff Blakely says.

"Badger'll be waitin' in the cell when you get back to Jarbidge," Percy says.

"Well, he better be," Sheriff Blakely says. "I won't make you come back to Jarbidge with us. Your horse is played out. But I ask that you stay here with John Gaar for a couple days. If Badger's not there, you, as his accomplice, go back in my jail."

"I'd be happy to take Percy in for a few days," Mr. Gaar says.

Percy wipes the sweat from his forehead and smiles in relief. Sheriff Blakely and his posse move off, riding their horses back toward Jarbidge. Percy sighs. *I'm in the clear,* he thinks. *I just hope Badger finds what he's lookin' for. If not, I hope he's still in Jarbidge.*

Chapter Seven

BADGER IS USED TO being bored. He was bored when he rode behind four hundred lazy steers. He was bored when he built a rock fence. Badger gets bored on those winter nights when it's just too cold to sleep but not cold enough to stoke the fire. But this is a totally different kind of boring.

Badger's mind spins through countless ways to present the evidence to Sheriff Blakely. If he just tells Sheriff Blakely that Frank Newton and Madeline Dubois did it, the sheriff will laugh at him again. Badger doesn't mind a good laugh, but he does mind being laughed at. Badger could try to get Frank to confess, but Frank would probably just keep his eyes closed. Maybe Badger could lie down next to Frank in the doctor's office and pretend he was knocked silly, too. They could have a possum contest to see who would give up playing hurt first. Badger really wants to get Mrs. Dubois to show her double-shot pistol to Sheriff Blakely, but he can't figure out how to do it without getting shot.

Badger fidgets in one of the uncomfortable bunks. Even though he's bored, his mind won't stop racing, so he can't fall asleep. What makes this boring different from his usual dull stretches of time is Badger's lingering fear that the door will burst open to reveal Mrs. Dubois standing at the backside of a rifle barrel.

He looks at the hole in the roof and daydreams about escaping. Badger thinks about heading south and joining Pancho Villa's army. He could ride the borderlands between Mexico and the US like the bandit he is beginning to feel like. This simple solution for him, however, would probably land Percy in prison. Badger can't do that to Percy.

Badger lies on his bunk and strains to listen to the activity outside. He hears the clank of hammers and pickaxes striking rocks at a nearby mine. He hears a couple dogs either fighting or playing. He's not sure which, but he thinks their ruckus is impressive. He hears wagons rolling slowly down the street past the jail. He hears the click, shuffle, click, shuffle of a woman walking quickly down the street. *A woman walking quickly!* Badger jumps up from his bunk. He places his ear against the cell wall to better hear the steps. They're getting closer. Badger crawls into a corner and rolls himself up like a baby foal, making himself as small of a target as he can. But he knows he is still a big target at close range.

Badger sweats like a washerwoman at a steamy laundry house. Sweat trickles down his face, and wet rings form where Percy's sleeves meet his shirt. Badger's heart beats in time with the click, shuffle, click, shuffle he hears rounding the jail's corner. In the sudden silence, Badger's heart skips a beat. The handle on the jail's exterior door turns slowly, and the door opens a few inches. Badger sees a shiny, black boot with frilly fringe slide inside, then a dress, and finally Mrs. Dubois.

He snaps his eyelids shut. The door closes sharply, but Badger refuses to look. He breathes quickly, hoping each breath isn't his last.

"Wake up, you untidy moron," Mrs. Dubois says through the steel door's window. "You have caused me a great deal of trouble, and I intend to clear up this mess right now."

"Please, don't shoot me!" Badger pleads as he begins to cry. "I'm too young to die."

"*Vous papillon floraison peu,*" Mrs. Dubois says with an evil chuckle.

Badger sniffles and wipes his eyes. "I don't know French," Badger says. "What does that mean?"

"I just called you a little crybaby," Mrs. Dubois says, "or I called you a flowering butterfly. I'm not sure. You see, I, uh, my pronunciation and syntax are impeccable, but my vocabulary is *moquent*, or is it *manquent*? I can't keep those straight. It's not the best."

"Well, I don't like bein' called a crybaby in any language," Badger says between whimpers. "I just wanna—"

"Shut up! Shut up! Shut up!" Mrs. Dubois snaps like an impatient schoolteacher. "I will do the talking; you will do the listening and nodding in agreement."

"Okay, okay, just please don't shoot me."

"Shhh. Mouth closed. I'm not shooting anyone. A lady does not kill," Mrs. Dubois says in a snotty tone. "A lady hires someone else to kill for her."

"But you said—"

"Why is your mouth open?" Mrs. Dubois interrupts. "You have a serious problem following directions."

"I'm sorry. I'll just—" Badger slaps his hand over his mouth.

"Here is my proposal," Mrs. Dubois says. "I have $600 left from my share of the robbery. I will pay you $25 to sneak out of jail and leave Jarbidge. You must never come back and must never talk to anyone about what happened on the stagecoach."

Badger pulls his hand away from his mouth and says, "All I have to do is leave, and you will pay me $25?"

"That is correct," Mrs. Dubois replies.

"I see how this is a good deal for me," Badger says, "but what's in it for you?"

"You are the only person who has figured out that Mr. Newton and I robbed the stagecoach," Mrs. Dubois says as she glares at Badger. "Mr. Newton and I were going to divide the money, $1,200 for me and $600 for him, but you ruined that by finding and returning my share to the sheriff. If you hadn't wrecked the plan, I would have gotten away from my husband and Mr. Newton could've quit working at that job he hates. But you can fix that all right now. If you escape and leave town, no one will be here to lay the blame at my feet. I get some money, and I get away with it. It is the cleanest alternative."

"And I spend the rest of my life on the run," Badger says as he shakes his head.

"At least you would still be alive!"

"I thought you said a lady doesn't kill."

"A lady *hires* someone else to kill for her," Mrs. Dubois says. "If you don't take the $25, I will offer it to Mr. Newton to kill you. He is scared of me and will do it. Either way, I win. But if Mr. Newton were to get the $25, the situation would be much messier—and you would be dead."

"I think you're bluffin'," Badger says as confidently as he can. "I don't think you have it in you. If you wanted to shoot me, you could've done it at your shack or even here."

"A lady never kills, you idiot!" Mrs. Dubois shrieks. She takes a deep breath and exhales slowly through her nostrils.

Badger senses her frustration.

"How many times do I have to tell you that? Nor does a lady bluff," Mrs. Dubois continues. "I have money, so I don't need to bluff. I can pay someone to kill you, just like I pay someone to wash my dress or style my hair. Your death would be nothing more than a business transaction to me."

"I'm just a business transaction to you?" Badger asks.

"You are nothing to me," Mrs. Dubois says coldly. "That is why your death, or you leaving, is just a business transaction."

Badger sits quietly for a moment. He liked being called a crybaby in French better than being called a business transaction. Badger realizes none of his choices is very good. *What happens if Percy has to come back to jail because I'm gone when the sheriff comes back?* Badger wonders.

"Why don't you just leave now?" Badger asks. "It would save you $25."

"I'm a lady," Mrs. Dubois replies. "A lady is never rushed. How would it look if I were to leave in a hurry? Everyone would think I had been involved in the robbery."

"But you *were* involved in the robbery," Badger says, frustrated.

"A lady must never—"

"Who comes up with all these lady rules?" Badger asks heatedly. "I'll take your money and get out of here."

"All right," Mrs. Dubois says as she opens her paisley handbag. She pulls out a twenty-dollar bill and five ones. "You are to leave immediately. Get out of town. And if I see you again, I might not treat you so lady-like."

Mrs. Dubois slips a delicate hand and wrist between the bars of the cell door's window. As Badger reaches for the money, she drops the bills and quickly retracts her hand. "A lady must never touch a commoner."

Badger picks up the money off the floor. He folds the crisp bills and places them carefully in Percy's shirt pocket. "I don't know much," Badger says angrily as Mrs. Dubois opens the jail's exterior door, "but I do know you're not a lady. You're a pig farmer. You aren't foolin' anyone with your money and your act."

"Insolence!" Mrs. Dubois yells as she steps outside, slamming the door behind her.

Badger presses his palms against his temples and crawls into his bunk again. He wants to cry like a little baby with a wet diaper, but instead he blinks away his tears. He must leave Jarbidge, but he doesn't want to land Percy in trouble. Badger leans back and covers his eyes. *What should I do?*

BADGER POKES HIS HEAD UP through the roof's loose tin. He carefully scans the area. The street out front is quiet. Badger looks behind the jail and sees the steep, brush-covered slope. With Jarbidge in a canyon, Badger feels like a field mouse waiting for a hawk to swoop down and snatch him. He climbs out and clumsily lowers himself to the ground. Badger tiptoes into the street and then hotfoots it toward the livery stables. If he wants out of Jarbidge, he needs a horse, and this time he has money.

Maybe Mr. Starlin' will have an idea about how to get out of Jarbidge without gettin' Percy into trouble, Badger thinks.

As Badger approaches the stables, he hears the familiar *clang, clang, clang* of the farrier at work. Gene bangs on a horseshoe like he's playing the cymbals in a marching band. The sound gets louder as Badger enters the structure.

"Hold still, you ring-tailed nincompoop!" Gene hollers at a blue-roan horse that is covered in tiny blue-gray spots. He strikes the nail twice more, setting the shoe in place. He quickly places a second nail and drives it into the hoof. The horse lifts his hoof slightly and swishes his tail.

"Stop movin', you bleary-eyed, grass-eatin' clown!" Gene yells.

He strikes the nail twice more and then drops the hoof to the ground. The horse stamps his foot and swishes his tail. Only then does Gene see Badger near the doorway.

"What can I help you with?" Gene asks.

"I need a horse," Badger says.

"To rent or to buy?" Gene asks, squinting his eyes at Badger. "Hey, aren't you the boy who stopped by earlier without any money?"

"I have money this time," Badger says. "I have $25."

"How'd you come up with that much money in so little time?" Gene asks. "You're not tryin' to spend stolen money with me, are you?"

"No, no, I didn't steal it."

"Then where'd you get it?"

"I got it from Mrs. Dubois. She gave it to me to leave town."

"Why does she want you to leave?"

"Because I'm the only person who knows—" Badger stops abruptly. He doesn't want to give away his secret.

Gene looks up suspiciously. "Knows what, Badger? Knows that she was involved in the robbery?"

Badger nods as he stares at the stables' dirt floor. He kicks a horse apple, realizing too late that it's fresh. He curls his lip in disgust and attempts to wipe the green slime off his boot's toe in the dirt.

"She offered me $25 to leave. She said if I didn't take it, she'd give Frank Newton $25 to kill me," Badger says as he chokes back a whimper.

"She's bluffin'," Gene says with a nod of his head.

"That's what I thought," Badger says a little too loudly, "but she said a lady never bluffs."

Gene laughs loudly. "Well, she's no lady."

"That's what I thought, too, but she's very convincin'."

"Madeline Dubois might want you dead," Gene says too casually for Badger's liking, "but Frank Newton surely wouldn't do it. He has a thing about killin'. One time, Frank rolled in here after runnin' over a ground squirrel. He was so upset he was almost in tears. And that was just over a squirrel."

"So you think I should just wait around?" Badger asks.

"I wouldn't. That crazy woman's mighty unpredictable. If she is this close to gettin' away with robbery, there's no tellin' what she might do."

"So what can I get for $25?" Badger asks.

"You could buy either that sorrel or the roan over there for $25," Gene says, pointing with his hammer. "Or you could buy the old brown with the star on his head and a saddle for $25, but I can't guarantee he'll make it out of the canyon."

"Well, I need a saddle, so I guess I'll take the brown," Badger says as he reaches into Percy's shirt pocket. He pulls out the bills, hands them to Gene, and forces a smile.

"Is this the stolen money?" Gene asks.

"I didn't steal it," Badger protests. "Mrs. Dubois gave this to me—"

"And she stole it from the mail stage?" Gene asks as he takes the cash.

Badger nods.

"I'll make sure Sheriff Blakely gets this," the farrier replies.

"But how can I get a horse and hightail it out of Jarbidge without that money?" Badger asks. He feels like he is talking to a fence post. *Mr. Starlin' just doesn't understand the trouble I'm in,* Badger thinks.

"Believe me, sonny, I know you're in a pickle. But I think we can figure something out that isn't just the easy way, but the right way."

Badger looks pained. He would prefer the easy way, or at least the way that would quickly put some dusty trails between him and Mrs. Dubois.

"Okay, Mr. Starlin'," Badger says after a pause. "What's my best chance for stayin' alive until Sheriff Blakely returns?"

"You know, I got to thinkin'," Gene says with a casual wink. "You got into this predicament because you work for the stagecoach company."

"Well, I *did* anyway," Badger says.

"Have you been fired yet?" Gene asks. "It's customary for someone to draw his wages when he gets fired."

"Well, no, I guess not. Frank is still pretendin' he got hit on the head. And the rest of the company is based in Rogerson." Badger pauses to think. "What do you have in mind, Mr. Starlin'?"

"Well, after the robbery, Sheriff Blakely brought the stage and team of horses here," Gene says. "If someone who works for the company were to come for the stage and horses, I'd have to give 'em up."

Badger shakes his head. "I know where you're headed with this, Mr. Starlin', and I think it's a bad idea."

"You haven't even heard my idea," Gene whines.

"Well, lemme tell you, I have never driven a one-horse buggy let alone a stagecoach with a four-horse team," Badger explains. "I don't even know how to hitch the team by myself or ready the wagon."

"I usually hitch the team for Frank when he's headin' out of town," Gene says excitedly. "I can do the same for you."

"But what about a driver?" Badger says. "I'm not gonna learn to drive a stage on Crippen Grade! I'd rather take my chances with Mrs. Dubois."

Gene sets down his hammer. He bends down and pulls six square nails out of a cuff in the leg of his overalls. He stands up and winces as he arches his back.

"You know what galls me most?" Gene asks.

"What's that, Mr. Starlin'?"

"I break my back every day to make a couple bucks," Gene growls. "Now don't get me wrong. I like what I do, and I'm not complainin', but I struggle for all I get. Then somebody like Madeline Dubois gets a little money and starts treatin' everybody like dirt. She thinks she can get away with any crime. And unless you do something about it, she will get away with robbery."

"Why are you so sure she's guilty and I'm innocent?" Badger asks.

"Because I know your type; you're not perfect, but you're true to yourself," Gene says. "And I know Madeline Dubois. She'd steal a nickel from a two-year-old if she thought it would improve her status."

Badger cracks a grin.

74

"Besides," Gene says with a toothy smile, "I know she wants to get out of town in a hurry. She brought her trunk and other luggage down here about an hour ago. They're already loaded in the stagecoach."

"But she told me a lady is never rushed," Badger says.

"And I told you she is no lady," Gene says. "She's in a rush but can't leave, because the company hasn't sent a driver to fetch the stage yet."

"Did you check her luggage?" Badger asks excitedly. "Is the stolen money in it?"

"Her trunk is locked tighter than a bear trap," Gene says. "But I don't think she'd go to the trouble of lockin' up just her boots and dresses."

"Why don't we break open the lock?" Badger asks. "If the stolen money is inside it, we could just wait here for the sheriff."

"No way am I breakin' into Madeline Dubois's luggage and then waitin' here while she's still in town," Gene says. "She's crazy, son, and I don't wanna be around when she gets madder than a half-skinned weasel."

"I still think this is a bad idea," Badger says, "but hitch up the team. I'll give it a try."

Gene hurries into a small room in the barn-like stables. He walks to the first stall and leads a brown horse out to the hitching pole just outside. He repeats the process with the other three horses.

The farrier places a collar over the first horse's head. He slides the collar down the beast's neck until it fits snugly against the horse's shoulders. Gene throws a saddle on the horse's back. It's not a riding saddle; it's a thick strip of leather with hooks and straps on it. Gene reaches under the horse, yanks the contraption's bellyband under the creature's chest, and tightens the saddle against the horse's back and belly. Next, the farrier pulls long wooden poles called traces through holes in the saddle and hooks the poles snugly to either side of the collar.

The horses fidget and stomp as they wait for Gene to finish up. The farrier outfits the other three horses in the same way he did the first. Then he slips bits into the horses' mouths and pulls bridles up over their ears.

"Let's get 'em hooked up," Gene says to Badger. "I'll get the two brown horses; you bring the sorrels."

Badger grabs the two big red horses' reins, leads them to the stagecoach, and walks them into place. Badger scratches his forehead as Gene latches each horse's traces to a short pole called the single tree just under each horse's tail. He then attaches the two trail horses' single trees to a double tree, the double tree to the tongue of the wagon, and the tongue to the stagecoach's axles. He follows the same procedure with the lead horses' single trees and another double tree. Gene pulls the jerk lines up onto the stagecoach and rests them over the dashboard.

Badger searches his brain for a way to convince Gene this is a bad idea. Nothing comes to mind, so Badger silently stands and stares at the waiting stagecoach.

Chapter Eight

"YOU'RE ALL READY TO go, Badger," Gene says as he pulls the last buckle tight.

Badger opens his mouth to speak and then hesitates. "This isn't a good idea, Mr. Starlin'," he finally says. "I'm not very good with one horse, much less four horses."

"You'll be fine," Gene says. "These horses could probably drive themselves."

"Then why don't I just sit in the passenger compartment?" Badger asks as he points to the stage's cabin.

"Jump up in the driver's seat," Gene says enthusiastically. "You'll do fine."

Badger clambers up the left, front wheel's spokes, pulls himself into the driver's seat, and carefully picks up the reins. The teen hefts them, adjusts his grip, and then adjusts his grip again. The eight strips of leather feel awkward to him. Badger sets the reins back over the dashboard and sits on his hands.

"I can't even hold the reins right," Badger whines.

"Get 'em all even, Badger," Gene says. "The reins for the two horses on your left go in your left hand, and the reins for the two on your right go in your right hand. Loop the lead horses' reins over your pointer fingers, and loop the trail horses' reins between your middle and ring fingers. Keep 'em all even, and make sure you have even pressure all the time. You have to tell all four horses the same command at the same time through those reins."

Badger pulls all the reins slightly taut and makes them even. He winds the reins through his fingers and grips them tightly.

"Don't hold 'em too tight," Gene says, "or your hands will cramp up."

Badger relaxes his grip and wonders about all the little hints Gene isn't telling him about. "Since you know what you're doin', why don't you drive the team?" Badger asks.

"I'm not a teamster," Gene says.

"What's a teamster?" Badger asks.

"Somebody who works for a company that runs a team of horses," Gene says. "I slap shoes on horses; that makes me a farrier. Teamsters and farriers have an understandin'. Teamsters won't touch a horse's hooves, and farriers won't sit in the driver's seat."

"But I'm not a teamster either," Badger says.

"You work for the stagecoach company," Gene says, smiling. "That makes you a teamster whether you like it or not."

The four horses stomp their hooves and impatiently wait for Badger's instructions. Badger pulls back on the reins to relax the beasts. The stagecoach shudders forward and back as the horses dance in place.

"Bad idea or not, we need to hit the road right now," Gene says excitedly.

"I'm not sure about this. I just—what do you mean by 'we'?" Badger asks.

Gene grabs his hammer and a chisel. He runs to the stagecoach, pulls its door open, and looks up at Badger. "I see Madeline Dubois walkin' this way, and she looks madder than a cow with a newborn calf. Now's not the time to be timid, Badger. Now is the time to drive."

Gene jumps in the stage and slams the door. Badger stands up and looks behind the coach. Mrs. Dubois's dress dances around her as she strides toward the livery. Spotting Badger, she reaches into her handbag and pulls out her pistol. She aims hastily and squeezes the trigger. Badger drops to the stagecoach's seat as the shot rings out.

The nervous horses all lunge forward at the same time. The collars pull tight, the trace lines pull tight, the double trees pull tight, and the stagecoach lurches forward. Badger is forced deeper into the seat as the stagecoach follows the scared team of horses. A second shot rings out, and Badger ducks. The young cowboy pulls back on the reins to slow the horses.

From beneath his seat, he hears Gene yell, "Just let 'em run, Badger! It'll get the fresh off 'em, and you won't wear yourself out tryin' to stop 'em."

Badger relaxes his grip but still maintains some upward tension on the reins to help keep him in his seat. The horses run wildly down the street. Badger pulls them to the right around a curve and then back to the left to round a second corner. The teen suspects the horses are ignoring his commands. Either way, he's glad they and all four wheels are staying on the road.

The team runs at a frantic pace for about a quarter mile. The horses slow as they approach Crippen Grade.

"Pull 'em back, Badger," Gene hollers from inside the cabin. "The grade turns up in about a hundred yards, and they'll run out of breath if we go this fast up the hill."

Badger pulls steadily on the reins. The horses ignore him. He pulls harder, but the horses stubbornly bite their bits so they can disregard Badger's commands.

In a deep, firm voice, Gene calls, "Whoa! Whoa, boys."

The horses quickly slow to a canter, then a trot, and finally a brisk walk. Badger pulls once more on the reins to remind the horses he is in charge and then slacks the reins. The horses and trailing stagecoach turn slightly right and begin heading up Crippen Grade. They walk up a steep slope for about one hundred yards. The road levels out, and Badger relaxes in his seat.

Gene pokes his head out the passengers' window and says, "Stop here, Badger. The horses need a rest. We don't wanna wear them out this early in the trip."

Badger pulls back on the reins and says, "Whoa. Whoa, boys."

The horses stop and breathe heavily. The stage is a little more than a mile outside Jarbidge. But after the steep climb, it is high above the town. Badger relaxes his grip and pushes forward on the brake lever to keep the wagon from rolling. He takes a nervous breath and looks back at Gene. As Badger turns, he notices a cloud of dust below them on the trail. He halfway stands, turns his head, and squints his eyes to catch a glimpse of the rider kicking up the dust. Atop the star-headed brown horse rides a woman whose long dress flaps with each stride. Badger is sure the rider is Mrs. Dubois, and he is sure she is mad.

"Uh, Mr. Starlin'," Badger says louder than necessary. "How long do the horses need to rest?"

"Five minutes would give 'em a chance to air out. Why're you askin', Badger?"

"Mrs. Dubois is comin' up behind us," Badger blurts out, "and she looks mad."

"I changed my mind," Gene says. "Let's go now."

Badger pulls back on the lever to release the brake. He quickly measures the reins and loops them over his fingers. Badger shakes the reins, and the horses strain against their burden. The wagon moves forward, and they all begin heading up the trail again.

"How fast can we go?" Badger asks without turning around.

"These horses can't pull much faster than a walk," Gene says. "Even though I'm scared of any angry woman with a gun, I'm more scared of Crippen Grade."

Badger flaps the reins to encourage the horses. He doesn't want them to go too fast, though, because the stagecoach could tip over. But if they don't go fast enough, Mrs. Dubois could catch up. And if she's reloaded her pistol, she'll have two chances to shoot him dead.

UP AHEAD, BADGER SEES a trail of dust—not the type the wind stirs up, but the kind horses kick up. Badger stands to get a better look. He strains his eyes. As the dust cloud nears, the young driver makes out six horses, all with riders.

"How many riders were in the sheriff's posse, Mr. Starlin'?" Badger asks.

"Let's see; the sheriff and four, no, five riders."

"Well, I think I see 'em," Badger says.

Glancing behind the stage, Badger realizes Mrs. Dubois is gaining ground. He looks down the steep-sided canyon. The stage is bouncing and swaying on the rocky road. *If this stagecoach tips over, it'll probably crash all the way to the canyon's bottom,* Badger thinks. He gulps and pulls back on the reins.

Badger looks back at Mrs. Dubois, who hastily fires her gun at him. The sound rings out, but Badger doesn't hear a bullet whiz past. He pulls on the reins, worried the team might bolt. He pulls again, and the winded horses stop.

"If we keep tryin' to outrun her, we'll kill these horses or fall into the canyon," Badger tells Gene. "She's fired three times and hasn't shot close even once. I think a pistol that small is only accurate at close range."

"You think so?" Gene asks. "Would you bet your life on it?"

84

"We can't outrun her," Badger says, his voice trembling in fear. "I just hope the sheriff gets here in time."

MRS. DUBOIS'S EYES BLARE with rage as she pounds her heels against her horse's belly to make him gallop faster. Meanwhile, Sheriff Blakely and his posse slow to a walk as they approach a treacherous corner. Badger wants to scream at them to hurry as they plod slower than the mounted sheriff's posse in the annual Independence Day parade.

Badger swallows hard to tame his churning stomach. His heart races, and his eyes dart around, searching for an escape route. *She's really gonna shoot me,* Badger thinks. He scans his brain for something witty to say, something that will make Mrs. Dubois pause long enough to give Sheriff Blakely time to arrive.

Mrs. Dubois charges her horse across the remaining twenty-five feet separating her from Badger. She stops abruptly and pulls her horse in a tight circle to calm him. The cloud of dust she kicked up overtakes her and the stagecoach, leaving behind a fine residue. Mrs. Dubois is slightly disheveled from the ride. Her face is dusty, except for a couple of lines where beads of sweat have washed the dust away. A few stray hairs have escaped from beneath her fancy hat. She holds her horse's reins in one hand and her pistol in the other.

"What are you doing, Badger Thurston?" Mrs. Dubois screams.

"Just what you told me to do. I'm leavin' Jarbidge," Badger says as calmly as he can.

"You have my belongings. And I never told you to leave with the stage," Mrs. Dubois says angrily.

"It was the only ride I could find," Badger says. "And I wanted to bump into Sheriff Blakely on my way out."

"You'll regret that decision," Mrs. Dubois says as she points her pistol at Badger and fires.

Badger hears a bullet zoom past him at the same time the pistol announces its delivery. His heart thumps painfully, and he leans backward and falls from the stage. He lands on his side and lies motionless on the ground. Badger struggles to take a breath. He feels dizzy and hurts everywhere.

Hearing the shot, the sheriff and his posse spur their horses into a quicker pace. Mrs. Dubois lowers her gun and notices the approaching mounts for the first time. Gene pops out of the coach, runs to Badger, and drops to his knees.

"Badger! Badger, can you hear me?" Gene asks anxiously. "Are you shot? Are you bleedin'? Where have you been hit?"

Badger winks at Gene and asks in whisper, "Is Sheriff Blakely close?"

Gene looks puzzled but nods.

"I think she missed," Badger whispers. "I thought if it looked like she shot me, it'd light a fire under the sheriff."

Gene smiles like a gambler who was dealt four aces. Badger's ears ring, and the side of his body he landed on throbs, but he is otherwise unharmed. Badger exhales and takes a deep breath. Just breathing has never felt so good.

"Well, whip my horse and call me a jockey," Sheriff Blakely says as he and his posse finally arrive. "What's goin' on here?"

Badger slowly stands, and Gene steps behind the stagecoach. Badger and Mrs. Dubois both begin speaking. But Mrs. Dubois is louder, closer to Sheriff Blakely, and more persistent, so Badger closes his mouth.

"These two men have stolen my belongings," Mrs. Dubois says. "I want my things back, and I want you to arrest them."

Sheriff Blakely looks inside the stagecoach. He looks to its right and left. He looks up on its roof.

"Just one problem, ma'am," Sheriff Blakely says. "There's only one boy here."

"Where did that filthy farrier go?" Mrs. Dubois chirps.

"I'm back here," Gene replies from behind the stage. "I was just unloadin' your luggage for you. This is your locked trunk, isn't it?"

Mrs. Dubois pauses. She isn't sure what scheme Gene has brewing. "It is mine," she cautiously says.

"I know that," Gene says, "because I loaded it for you. I just wanted you to admit it to the sheriff for me."

"What's goin' on, Gene?" Sheriff Blakely asks.

"You might wanna see what's inside, Sheriff," Gene says casually. Gene pulls the chisel and hammer from his pocket. He places the chisel against the lock and strikes the chisel twice with the hammer. The lock breaks, and he lifts up the lid.

Badger peers inside the trunk. He sees blouses, skirts, boots, and some unmentionables. But he doesn't see any money.

"Why should I be interested in Mrs. Dubois's laundry, Gene?"

"She has the money," Badger blurts out. "She has a pistol that only fires two shots, just like at the robbery. She paid me to escape and leave town. She and Frank Newton worked together to steal the money so she could leave her husband and Frank could stop runnin' the stage for his father. Frank isn't hurt. Tickle his nose; that's what I did to wake him up. Frank got Mr. Greene out of the stage with some well-placed coffee. Then they got me off the stagecoach with the runaway. I just figured out that last part after discoverin' a short run like that tires out the horses and they have to stop. Anyway, when they stopped, Mrs. Dubois pulled the mailbags off the stage and stashed them in some bushes back up the road."

"Lies! Lies! He is a thief and a liar!" Mrs. Dubois yells. "Arrest them, Sheriff! Hurry, before they disturb my things."

As she is speaking, Gene tips her trunk over. Atop all her finery lands a small pink bag. Gene picks it up, peeks inside, and tosses the pouch to Sheriff Blakely. "You might wanna see this, Sheriff," Gene says.

The sheriff catches the bag and looks inside. He extracts the folded green papers and counts it.

"Five hundred seventy-five dollars," the sheriff says, looking at Mrs. Dubois.

"And Mr. Starlin' has the other $25," Badger says. "She gave it to me to leave town. I gave it to him for safe keepin'."

"This is all Frank Newton's fault," Madeline Dubois pleads. "All I did was move the money off the stage. Mr. Newton carried it to town. I was just holding the money for him. A lady doesn't steal."

"A lady gets someone else to steal for her," Badger says with a smirk. "And you're no lady."

"Well, burn my toast and call me hungry," Sheriff Blakely says as he walks over to Mrs. Dubois. "It's all clear now. Madeline Dubois, you're under arrest for robbin' the Jarbidge mail stage and for tryin' to shoot Badger Thurston dead."

Sheriff Blakely takes the pistol out of her hand. He helps Mrs. Dubois off her horse and slaps handcuffs on her wrists. He leads her to the stagecoach and looks up at Badger.

"Badger, could you please drive the coach back to Jarbidge for me? Mrs. Dubois needs a ride to my jail. And I need to get back to have a little talk with Frank Newton."

"I was plannin' on headin' on back to Rogerson," Badger says as he points to the east.

"I don't think so," Sheriff Blakely says. "You sneaked out of my jail again. I'm not gonna put you in irons, but you owe me another night. Since there's only one cell, though, you'll have to stay at my house."

Badger chuckles ruefully. He jiggles the reins and pulls the horses around. The stagecoach turns a tight circle, and Badger stops it long enough to let Mrs. Dubois in the coach. Gene catches the brown horse Mrs. Dubois had been riding, swings onto his back, and joins the caravan heading back to Jarbidge.

Sheriff Blakely turns to Badger and says, "I had you figured all wrong, Badger, and I'm sorry. Mrs. Blakely makes a really good berry pie. I'll ask her to bake one for you tonight. You did escape from my jail, but you have earned my respect."

Badger smiles at the sheriff. He nods his head and shakes the reins. The horses jump to a start, and the stagecoach rolls down the trail.

GLOSSARY

alibi—being somewhere else than the place a crime is committed.

axle—the bar shaft connecting the wheels to a car or wagon.

bay horse—a brownish red horse with a black mane and tail.

bit—the part of a bridle that goes in a horse's mouth.

blue-roan horse—a horse hide color that is created from a mixture of black, grey and white hair.

boomtown—a rapidly growing town or district.

bridle—a device worn on a horse's head used to guide and control the horse.

buckboard—a type of wagon

buggy—a type of wagon

circuit judge—a judge that moves his court from town to town.

customary—actions holding to socially agreed upon customs or unwritten laws.

desperado—a western outlaw.

disheveled—a messed up appearance.

evidentiary hearing—a court appearance to determine if there is enough evidence for a trial.

farrier—a person that cares for a horse's feet. Someone who puts horseshoes on horses.

fetlock—the tuft of hair just above the back of the hoof on a horse.

gallery—the audience seating at a trial.

gallows—used for hanging condemned prisoners.

guffaws—a loud laugh.

hightail—when a horse or cow is scared, they will run with their tail high in the air.

horse apple—horse manure.

insolent, insolence—someone who is insulting or disrespectful.

jerk lines—the reins used to control a horse hitched to a wagon.

kerchief—a head or neck covering.

livery stables—where horses are rented, sold, or stabled in a town.

Panco Villa—a famous general in the Mexican revolution from 1910 to 1920. He conducted raids along the US-Mexican border which included raids into the United States.

pincers—a tool with two handles and two jaws that works on a pivot and is used for grabbing things, in this case hot horseshoes.

posse—volunteers helping a sheriff for a specific task.

reprobates—a depraved or unprincipled person. Someone who is unworthy.

riding shotgun—on a wagon, the man sitting next to the driver with a shotgun, protecting the wagon.

smitten—to affect someone with passion or emotion

sorrel horse—a red haired horse.

splayed—feet and legs wider than the body.

spokes—wooden linkages between the inner and outer portions of a wagon wheel.

stagecoach—a type of wagon.

steam engine—an old fashioned engine that runs from steam. Coal or wood is burnt to heat water until it steams, and the pressure from the steam turns a motor.

tailor—someone who sews or makes clothing.

teamster—someone who drives a wagon.

tepid—moderately warm

three-pole fence—a fence made of a post with three wood poles between each post.

traces—two straps, chains or poles attached to a harness and used to attach a horse to a wagon.

two-track road—A road created by wagon traffic. The road has two tracks side-by-side where a horses walk and the wheels of the wagon roll.

From the author...

Badger Thurston and the Runaway Stagecoach is a work of fiction. But aspects of this book are based on real history. In the 1910s, Jarbidge, Nevada, was one of the last mining boomtowns in the continental United States. It was a thriving town, and more than one thousand people lived there.

On December 5th, 1916, the mail stage carrying $4,000 in payroll for the mine laborers was late. A search party was formed, and what they discovered shocked the whole community. Fred Searcy, the stagecoach's driver, was found murdered, and the mail sacks carrying the money were missing.

Following an investigation, Ben Kuhl was arrested and tried for murder and robbery. With District Attorney Edward Carville prosecuting the case, Kuhl was convicted and sentenced to life in prison. Carville later became governor, and he pardoned Kuhl. Locals claim the Jarbidge stage robbery of 1916 was the last stage robbery in the United States.

About the Author...

Gus Brackett is a lifelong cowboy. He was raised on his family's ranch and has worked on that same ranch since 1998. He graduated from Utah State University in 1998 and earned a Master's in Business Administration from Northwest Nazarene University in 2001. Gus currently resides with his wife and four children on their cattle ranch in southwest Idaho.

Made in the USA
Lexington, KY
10 February 2014